GIVE:
AN ANTHOLOGY OF
ANATOMICAL ENTRIES

EDITED BY MICHELLE KILMER AND T.J. TRANCHELL

PETER,
YOU ARE THE BEST PERSON
SIGNED,
DEFINITELY T.J.

ISBN: 0988252295
ISBN-13: 978-0-9882522-9-5

TO THE ORGAN DONORS, FOR GIVING LIFE

TABLE OF CONTENTS

GIVE:
AN ANTHOLOGY OF
ANATOMICAL ENTRIES

EDITED BY MICHELLE KILMER AND T.J. TRANCHELL

SAMRAT
BY JONATHAN LAMBERT

Samrat sat on a packed train as it rolled toward the Tirupati station in Andhra Pradesh, South India, considering what to pray for after he was tonsured, or shaved, at the Tirumala Venkateswara Temple. He waited until his twenty-fifth birthday to make this pilgrimage to offer his long and lustrous black hair to Lord Venkateswara, and he didn't want to pray for something silly.

He knew he should have embarked on this pilgrimage two years earlier, when he was still the secret love of his beautiful Urmila. He would have prayed that somehow their parents could see beyond the difference in caste and allow them to marry. He would have been a great husband to her. Much better than that donkey-ass, Lakshman, whom her parents arranged for her to marry last year. It was too late to pray about that.

Lakshman knew that Samrat loved Urmila and never missed an opportunity to taunt him. He even threatened to kill Samrat on several occasions if he didn't stay away from her.

Samrat chose to make the pilgrimage now because he had no focus or purpose in his life since Urmila's marriage. He was going nowhere, and he hoped the donation of his hair at the temple, along with prayers, would help him find a new path. The temple took the hair from almost twenty thousand pilgrims per day, selling it overseas where it became wigs and hair extensions.

Once he arrived at Tirupati, he went to a counter and got a wristband indicating the time to get in line for his tonsure. He then took a bus directly to the town of Tirumala and arrived at the temple.

After a long wait, he found himself sitting cross-legged on the floor before a temple barber who was armed only with a sharp knife, towel, and a bowl of water. He lowered his head. The barber was fast and efficient.

His tonsure done, Samrat cleansed himself and made his way into the inner sanctum, feeling his newly bald head. It felt odd without all the hair.

In the inner sanctum, he offered a silent prayer to Lord Venkateswara, an avatar of Vishnu.

Lord Venkateswara, please bless me with peace and prosperity. He paused, then added, *And please cause the death of Lakshman Kakkar.*

Where that came from he didn't know, but once voiced, he couldn't take it back.

*

He returned to Chennai in the same manner. A week later, he happened upon none other than Lakshman Kakkar.

"Samrat! I heard you went on a pilgrimage, and now I see from your head that you did. Did you pray to get a life and get out of mine?"

"Something like that. How are you feeling by the way?"

"It's funny you should ask. Don't know if you were aware that I was diagnosed with cancer?"

Samrat smiled to himself. *Yessss,* he thought. *Thank you Lord Venkateswara! There is hope for Urmila and me after all.*

"I was diagnosed shortly after getting married. I refused chemotherapy, but I did pray about it. Today I am happy to announce that, as of last week, I'm miraculously cancer free!"

Samrat was visibly shaken.

"Samrat? Are you okay?"

"Yes. Yes. Just shocked to hear this. I didn't know you had cancer." Samrat recovered.

"Well, no need to be shocked. All is well now. But I must get to my lovely wife. She's been so horny lately." Lakshman winked at him. "I'll see you soon."

Samrat continued on his way to work, now very depressed. He needed to forget about Urmila and get on with his life.

*

As his hair began to grow out, Samrat was certain it felt different than before. Rubbing his hand over the stubble gave him a strange suspicion that his hair was feeling him back. *Creepy*, he thought. Still, he figured it was just a normal sensation for someone recently tonsured.

He reconsidered that notion two months later when he banged his head on the kitchen cabinet. It hurt, but this was different. His head throbbed at the spot where the cabinet door connected with his skull, but the pain radiated up the strands of his now spiky hair. It was awful. He fell to his knees, clutching his hair. Touching it caused even more pain. He dropped his hands and sat down, waiting for the ache to pass. Samrat took extreme measures from that moment on not to touch or molest his hair in any way.

For the most part, other aspects of his life remained normal. He was dismayed to see Lakshman becoming more and more prosperous. He moved with Urmila to a fancy new condominium. He purchased an expensive car and showed it off around town. Samrat watched, and became ashamed for his wish, his prayer. It had backfired.

His hair reached his neck before he knew it. It was growing faster than before his pilgrimage. In less than a year, it brushed his shoulders. The length was fine with him, but it had a life of its own. It moved on its own volition. It slithered around his head in the shower. Hair products irritated it. Only baby shampoo was tolerable.

He tried to get a haircut, but the first snip of the scissors caused such intense pain that he screamed aloud. Blood dripped from the ends of the strands. Blood oozed from the cut strands on the floor. The barber shied away from him, calling him a demon and a *rakshasa*, and ordered him to leave the shop.

Samrat was a sea of emotions. Frightened and confused. Horrified and frustrated. He was still ashamed by the prayer at his pilgrimage. Still certain it had backfired. Lakshman was healed. If he had only known he was ill, he could have waited for him to die, and then Urmila would have been his.

He told no one about the problem with his hair. He was afraid that they would think he was a demon just like the barber had. He never tried to get it cut again so it continued to grow. Soon it was down to the middle of his back. If he was outside for any length of time, his hair got sunburnt and caused him days of misery. It wasn't long before he fell ill and simply stayed in his bed. Even that was no comfort. Just laying his head on the pillow gave him the sensation of pins and needles in his hair after a few minutes. He was miserable.

Once he got sick, his parents doted on him. They were very worried about him. He couldn't tell them what was wrong, just that he believed himself cursed.

This curse concerned them greatly. They called on the family guru, Swami Govindachari Sastrigal, to give Samrat advice.

"No, Mother. I don't want to talk to him."

"You must Samrat. He can help you. I'm beside myself seeing you like this. Please. Talk to him. It can't hurt and it might help. Please, Samrat, do it for me."

Samrat rolled his eyes. "Fine. Just for you."

"Thank you," his mother said, placing her hand on the top of his head and running it through his hair. Her hand felt very nice to him, maybe even too nice. He was aware of a scandalous stirring in his groin.

"Mother. Please stop. Go call the Swami before I change my mind."

*

Swami Govindachari Sastrigal peered inside Samrat's bedroom. He saw a young man in torment. Samrat looked pale, sick. The Swami was immediately concerned. He entered the room and approached

Samrat's bedside.

"Samrat?"

"Yes, Swami-ji. Good to see you."

"It is not good to see you, especially looking like this. What has happened?"

"I am cursed, Swami-ji."

"Tell me all."

Samrat told the Guru everything, including his illicit love of Urmila and his death wish prayer. The Guru was not pleased.

"Samrat. You are indeed cursed. A prayer for someone else's death—I have never heard of this before. It's all coming back on you. It is Karma. You must make amends before it is too late."

"But how Swami-ji? How can I make amends?"

"You must take the pilgrimage again. This time with a pure heart and a pure mind."

"How can I do that? My hair is alive. It bleeds when cut, and the pain—I can't even describe the pain."

"This is your punishment, Samrat. You must suffer through this again, willingly and gladly. Then you are giving true sacrifice and may receive the consideration you ask for. Book your trip right away. I will discuss this with your parents and if you require financial support, it shall be provided."

"Thank you Swami-ji. You are wise, and I will commit myself to this task and speak to you again when it is complete."

The Swami nodded to Samrat. He was still concerned about him, but if Samrat completed this second pilgrimage, the Swami thought maybe he would be okay.

*

The trip was booked, and soon Samrat found himself on the same train route to Tirumala. This time he didn't have the ambiguity he experienced on the previous trip. He knew exactly what he would pray for. After getting his wristband at Tirupati, he got on the bus to Tirumala. He remained calm, trying not to think of how much anguish he was about to endure.

When it was his turn to take his place to be tonsured, he sat down cross-legged and locked eyes with the barber. It was the exact same one that had shaved him before. This was fortunate.

"Excuse me sir, before you start. You probably don't remember me, but you did tonsure on me some time ago."

"I remember you."

"When I was here last time, I received a curse due to my foolish and selfish prayer. My hair is alive. When you cut it, it will bleed. Yet I must do this again, so please don't stop when it bleeds. No matter how much I scream. I must make amends."

The barber nodded and raised the knife.

The first cut was the worst. Samrat howled in agony as his hair dropped onto the floor beside him. The second cut was the worst. Samrat's shriek filled the temple. His eyes leaked tears and he hovered at the edge of consciousness. The barber grabbed his chin and stared into his wet eyes.

"You must not pass out if you are trying to reverse a curse. You must feel it all, all the pain, and reflect on it."

Samrat nodded and the knife rose again. The third cut, surely, was the worst. Samrat shuddered and began to fully cry. Blood from his hair was flowing down his face and coating his shirt.

A pause occurred in the temple as other pilgrims stopped to look at Samrat. They couldn't help but hear him scream, and now people loitered behind him, watching the horror show.

The fourth cut was the worst. The fifth cut was the worst. Each cut was successively more painful than the last. Blood was everywhere. Samrat felt as if he was in Naraka—in Hell. Would it ever end? He forced himself to focus on each slice of his hair, each scrape of his scalp. He bit deep into his tongue, causing more blood to join with the legion of rivulets running down his face. His previously white clothing had turned red, as did at least half of the barber's clothing.

Finally, it was finished. He was bald once again. Samrat stood on shaky legs and thanked the barber. The show was over, and the crowd dispersed. Now saturated and dripping blood even from his fingertips, he staggered in obvious distress on his way to cleanse himself prior to entering the inner sanctum.

Samrat performed a ritual purification and changed into a spare set of clothes he had brought. In the inner sanctum, again he offered a silent prayer to Lord Venkateswara.

Lord Venkateswara, I have offended you, and I have offended myself and others. I ask you now for my swift death. I cannot suffer like this, and I know I have done wrong. Please, Lord, end my suffering.

*

He left the temple by bus and boarded the return train to Chennai. Once aboard, he finally yielded to his suffering and passed out. When the train arrived at the station, his parents were waiting for him. They carried him to their car, and took him home. When he finally woke many days later, he saw his mother sitting by this bed.

"Samrat, you are awake. We've been so worried about you."

"Hello, Mother. I have made amends."

"What did you pray for? Is the curse lifted?"

"It will be. I prayed for a swift death."

"SAMRAT! NO!" she cried.

"It's okay, Mother, I deserve it."

"No Samrat, no. This cannot happen, especially after Lakshman's death. Our colony cannot take this much tragedy."

Samrat perked up.

"What? Lakshman died?"

"Yes. Cancer. They said he was cured, but when you were on your trip, he suddenly died, full of cancer. Doctors these days, they seem so smart but they know nothing."

Samrat reached up and touched his head. There was no more pain. He sat up. Energy rushed through him. Vitality. Vigor. He blinked his eyes several times and pinched himself to make sure he wasn't dreaming. He wasn't. He jumped out of bed.

"Samrat, take it easy. You are not well."

"Mother, I am very well." He kissed his mother on the forehead and went to his closet, quickly dressing.

"Where are you going, Samrat?"

"To pay my respects to Lakshman's family. I'll be back soon Mother. Don't worry." He ran over to her and kissed her forehead again before slipping out the door.

Samrat couldn't care less about Lakshman. *Cock-blocker*, he thought. *He deserved what he got.* He headed to Urmila's colony, and once he arrived, he called her on his cell phone.

"Urmila, I am outside. Can I come up?"

"Samrat, have you heard the news? Lakshman has died."

"Why do you think I am here?"

"Please, come up."

Once inside, he noticed Urmila no longer had a red bindi dot, a traditional custom to signify marriage, on her forehead. He embraced her and kissed her. She kissed him back.

Samrat smiled. The biggest smile of his life.

"It will still be frowned upon, but now that I am a widow, I will be able to marry you, different caste or not. If you still want me, that is. But you have to grow your hair back. I don't like a bald head."

Samrat could feel something growing. This time, it wasn't his hair.

"Don't worry. I will never get a haircut again. And I still want you. Very much!" He smiled at her.

"Then let's celebrate!"

She took his hand and led him to the bedroom.

Thank you, Lord Venkateswara.

ABOUT JONATHAN LAMBERT

Jonathan Lambert was born (and subsequently raised) in Maryland and now lives with his wife and two teenagers (God help him) in Virginia. During the day, he works as a Systems Analyst in

Washington, DC. That's all he can say about his work. At least that's what he told us. He probably works for the IRS and doesn't want you to know. He is a lifelong fan of horror genre, and has several stories published in other anthologies as well as a few self-published titles. He usually writes horror comedy, but sometimes he also writes funny horror, and on rare occasions, dark humor. He wants to write a novel, but probably never will. One can dream, however.

AG-327
BY ALEX KIMMELL

Joel easily recognized me as weaker prey and pounced day after day. Nothing the principal, teachers or parental figures used as threats slowed the marching intensity of his violence. School years slumped onward marked only by a relentless succession of bruises, torn clothes, broken bones, stolen lunch money, scars as reminders of my helplessness and the increasing vehemence of his cruelty's creativeness.

One winter morning in sixth grade stood sentinel against sleep for years. I'd created a winding path as a beat down buffer zone in an attempt to walk to school in relative peace. Mapped out through a period of trial and error, it served me well for a semester or two. On this particular day, whether by happenstance or an unexpected display of observation by Joel, I turned past the horse farm a block from the crosswalk and there he stood. A half-smoked cigarette squeezed between snarling lips and the usual herd of nasty sidekicks standing in a row behind him.

Before I turned to flee, he ripped my Star Wars backpack off and threw me into the hillside of bushes. The following only exists as blurred images in my mind. A broken branch— covered in blood from the corpse of a half-eaten squirrel—scratching into my cheek, the tip of a ballpoint pen etching misspelled curse words deep into my forehead and the hard, round bone of his knee grinding into my groin.

Bloodied, bruised and trembling, I readied my pencil on the notebook for Mr. Gavreau's lesson. Even in this state, I knew things would be better here than if I turned back for home and Dad's belly full of Jim Beam. Once again Nurse Randall had cleaned me up as best she could. Mouth too sore for the offered lollipop; I shook my head, unable to recall the license plate of the hit and run car.

*

By the time we made it to freshman year, Joel outweighed me by more than fifty pounds. He'd learned new and more potent techniques on the wrestling team before he was kicked off for dirty play. Without referees or evidence, Joel had no need of a conscience to keep him from hurting others, if he even had a conscience in the first place. I spent most downtime between classes in the library or sitting in the front office reading. When five minutes to bell ticked, my stomach lurched in time with the clock works. Every day, no reason ever given, the pain descended on me accompanied by the sickening melody of his hateful laughter.

Emergency room bills piled up along with the need for replacement clothing. The problem eventually grew too intense for my parents to bear. When summoned to the office, I refused to name names. Point of fact, by my senior year of high school, I stopped speaking all together.

*

Shortly after a particularly vicious beating, the Tall Man arrived at our door. Tailor made to his measurements, his suit was a second skin. His reassuring grin and twinkling eyes paved through Mom's defenses. She welcomed him inside to sit in the living room. Dad drank his nightly Tom Collins, Mom left her latest knitting project in its basket, and I pressed yet another icepack to my swollen eye socket as we listened to his proposition.

"It's not very often we find someone as gifted as your son." The Tall Man in the suit spoke slowly, his deep voice a warm baritone filling spaces in the air we never knew were empty in the first place. "IQ results *far* above anything we hoped to find. Obviously his exceptional GPA and extracurricular science activities caught our eye immediately."

My cheeks flushed behind the cold, dripping plastic bag.

"Have you chosen a school yet?" Though he must already have known the answer, I shook my head. "I would think you could go wherever you like."

"Never applied," I mumbled.

"Why is that?"

"He knows better. I ain't paying for some pipe smokin', snooty commie in a sweater vest to fill his head with jibber jabber," Dad barked. "He'll work in the shop with me and take over when I'm gone."

My family had owned the Broken Bottle Beverage Barn for four generations. I'd been helping in the storeroom after school ever since I could lift a box.

"Sir…" The man smiled, leaning forward on the edge of the crackly plastic that covered the love seat.

"Good enough for me, good enough for him." The tone of finality left no bones about Dad's opinion on the subject.

"I respect that, sir." The man slapped an open palm on his knee gently. "What about serving his country? Judging by the photos behind you I believe you're a former Marine?"

"Semper Fi." Dad tipped his tall glass in a lazy salute.

"We are an independent, fully functioning branch of the military. A privately-funded research division working to be sure that in these uncertain times, America continues her proud tradition of democracy, remaining the beacon of light she has always been." I could almost hear the marching drums and soaring brass band swell behind him.

"All we require is a small donation which will demonstrate your son's patriotism and devotion to this great nation of ours." The man leaned back, femininely crossing right leg over left, ankle down with a pursed-lipped grin. Judging Dad's body language, the decision was all but certain.

"How much do you need?" Dad flicked a finger at Mom to bring his checkbook.

"I'm sorry, but you misunderstand, sir. It isn't money we're looking for." The man pressed his round-knuckled middle finger against his temple. "What we need is in here."

"You won't get much out of his brain unless it's math or some sciency crap." Dad never was very complimentary.

"Oh, I believe his brain contains *exactly* what we need." The Tall Man narrowed his already thin eyes at me, hiding his pupils completely from view.

*

Of course my parents went for it. My eighteenth birthday wouldn't arrive for another four months, so the decision rested in their clutching hands. Mom consistently followed along with whatever Dad said. I never had a choice in steering the ship of my life at all. When Dad said turn starboard, we went starboard. No diversion from the course, no questions asked...*or else.*

The next morning they came for me. I climbed into the black sedan and sat next to the Tall Man. With no acknowledgment of my presence, we drove beyond the edge of town.

I don't really know what happened next or how long the procedure took. I do have one vague memory of a gas mask. Piercing, the recovery room's white light burned into my eyes, rousing me back to consciousness.

After my procedure, changes manifested immediately. My step grew more confident, quicker with unwavering intention. I raised my hand in class if I knew the answer. I'd even said no to Dad a couple times. His handprint marked the back of my neck and sides of my head for a few days, but I didn't mind. It was worth it.

When cornered by Joel, as his normally easy prey, I fought back. I don't mean blocked punches and feeble attempts to throw clumsy kicks. I accepted his knuckles to my eye sockets and cheekbones. I welcomed knees to my stomach and ripped out clumps of hair. Whereas before, the sight of my blood might have brought on tears and the fetal position, now it unleashed the wild.

I didn't stop with simple thrown fists or launching feet. I

thrust fingers in deep until his eyeballs popped. A sharpened pencil became my weapon, puncturing soft inner ear tissue and driving deep into gray matter. Nose cracked and throat crushed beneath my white rubber sneaker soles, splattering them with deep red. My forehead pounded repeatedly into his rib cage until bones ground into the heart, preventing the muscle from beating any further.

I didn't stop at hurting. I devastated. T-shirt smeared with traces of skin and bone, I swiped dripping bangs from my forehead, calmly returned to class, placed the previous night's homework on top of Mr. Gavreau's green blotter-covered desk, and sat in my assigned front center seat to read our next history chapter.

Screams and gasps of shock flowed into the room from the hallway. I smiled. Mr. Gavreau stared at me from the doorway, his face pale and trembling. I waved. He turned, vanishing from view. I don't know where he went. I heard he hasn't returned to school since.

Little fanfare. No bus ride home. A squad car ride to the station. Square jaws in olive green uniforms with weapons drawn in my direction, step-marched their echoing boots through the hall to escort me away. White lab coats leaned shoulder to shoulder, scrolling through photographs of bloodied locker doors on their glowing tablets. Metal cuffs fastened around my wrists and ankles with a short, extremely thick chain linking my neck to the scarred gray wall behind me.

Whispering voices in the hallway never referred to me by name. "The subject" and "the patient" were repeated in hushed tones. None of them seemed pleased.

"Hello, son." A White Coat stopped one step into the room. Two mountain-sized, weapon-wielding, camouflaged giants stood at his sides, fingers never drifting far from triggers. "How are you feeling?"

"Fine, thanks." I decided against describing the ray of sunshine radiating in my belly, shining since the moment I'd put my enemy out of my misery. "How are you?"

"Well, to be honest, we're all a bit in shock." He swiped

across his tablet screen. I read the bold-faced letters, "AG-327". White Coat followed my line of sight and flipped the device away from view. "You had quite a morning at school."

"Looks that way."

"Do you remember what you did to that boy?" Crossed arms held the tablet flat against his chest.

"Of course I do. What about it?"

"Does it make you feel bad or upset at all?"

"Not really." I dug a finger to rub between the collar and my neck. Tightening grips on their rifles, the soldiers secured battle-ready postures. "Son of a bitch deserved worse than what he got."

"Hmm. I see." White Coat tapped something into his tablet. "Were you frightened?"

I shook my head.

"Are you scared now?" He observed me pulling against the cuffs.

"Should I be?"

"You're chained to a wall and guarded by armed soldiers." He waved his hand at the guards. Blood dripped from my twisting, scraped wrists. "You haven't even asked who I am or where we are."

"Don't much care. I think I've been here before anyway." My words garbled as I leaned forward, links taut between my neck and the wall. I pulled at the metal rings now warm and wet. The soldiers aimed their weapons and I smiled. "It's the science smell. Kind of difficult to forget."

"Stand down," White Coat ordered the soldiers. After a brief hesitation, the guns once again pointed at the floor. "You can't break those chains, son."

"I know." I leaned back releasing the pressure against my throat. After a few deep breaths, I licked the open wound on my right wrist. My blood tasted much blander than I remembered. "What's AG-327?"

"You are." White Coat nodded.

"I am?"

"Technically it's the name of the procedure you went through to remove your…" He scratched his head.

"It's okay." I twined my fingers. "You took the fear part out of my brain."

"In non-scientific terms, yes." His index finger swiped at the screen quickly. Finding the page he needed, he turned the tablet so I could see. "We've been studying fear response in apes for nearly a decade now. Open cranial testing has steered us directly to the area…here." He pointed at a small glowing speck in a vaguely head-shaped blob.

"This is the MRI image of your brain before the procedure in which we removed section AG-327 from the Amygdala." His finger pushed the scan to the left of the screen. A new, practically identical picture took its place. "This is after we finished."

"Looks the same to me." I rubbed the top of my head. "Where are my scars? You didn't even shave my head."

"No need. Your skull remained intact." White Coat puffed his chest with pride. "The technique we developed is nearly non-invasive. After we put you to sleep, our machines remotely-controlled the microscopic camera and surgical tools through your eye…"

"I don't need the gory details, Doc." I stood. The soldiers' shoulders twinged. "I'm not scared anymore. That's what matters."

"That's why you…" He swallowed hard. "That's why you fought back this morning?"

"Yeah." I spun around, the wall cracking behind me. A large, jagged section of concrete with bolts and snapped edges of rebar spiking out tore free. I whipped my head forward feeling wind from the heavy projectile blow close to my ear. Before he could react, the slab crunched into the left soldier's face, breaking bone and scattering teeth to the floor.

White Coat released a high-pitched squeal at the sight of his own blood. A shard of soldier cheekbone drove into his shoulder, dropping him to his knees. I held my hands above my head, diving to the floor. With a loud crack, a bullet tore through the chain linking them together. More bullets chewed into the space I no longer occupied. Chunks of flooring exploded upward while I took the fallen soldier's rifle.

Two bursts of discharged ammunition were followed by a grunt, the clatter of plastic and metal on concrete, and then the smack of lifeless meat. I stood again, looking down at the two dead soldiers and the whimpering scientist.

"You took my fear." I straddled his trembling legs. "What you don't realize," I tapped my toe in the spreading blood as it poured from his shoulder, "is that you freed me from so much more." Bending low at the knees, I held myself just above his legs and looked him directly in the eyes. "Thank you, Doctor Sciency Man. I can't tell you how much I appreciate it."

"You...you're welcome." He puffed a heavy sigh through trembling lips. Despite the excruciating pain from his wound, the relief spreading from his face was palpable. He flinched as I placed my palms on the sides of his sweating cheeks. I pressed my lips to his forehead. He groaned quietly.

The neck cracked leaving his head hanging limply to the side.

"You stay here. I'm going home to thank my folks for this wonderful opportunity to show our patriotism."

Patting my hand against his rubbery cheek, my voice answered in echoes down the long hallway.

ABOUT ALEX KIMMELL

alex kimmell is a former (<u>NOUN</u>) from los angeles with a uniquely skewed (<u>ADJECTIVE</u>) on the dark side of the (<u>NOUN</u>). his first book "the Key to everything" is an amazon bestseller and has (<u>VERB</u>) the (<u>NOUN</u>) out of horror lovers around the (<u>NOUN</u>). his short fiction has appeared in publications by dynatox ministries, black lantern press, front row lit, canyon voices and the wordcount podcast as well as contributing words of (<u>ADJECTIVE</u>) to dumb

white husband and other (<u>PLURAL NOUN</u>) on the www. currently
he lives in rhode island with his family and two dogs that have very
short (<u>PLURAL NOUN</u>).you can find more information about his
(<u>NOUN</u>) and other (<u>ADJECTIVE</u>) psychosis at alexkimmell.com

SOUND AND SILENCE
BY KERRY G.S. LIPP

I heard about the explosion on my way to work. My hour commute was about the only rest I got, and now the newscast was bringing me down with yet another tragedy sure to claim the lives of several innocents.

Gas leak, terrorists, bad wiring, it didn't matter. People that didn't deserve it were dead, dying, and the survivors crippled for life.

I turned off the radio. I thought I'd get bored with the silence, but I didn't. It was therapeutic, almost cleansing, especially compared to the aural assault that made up the majority of my waking hours.

I thought about that as I pulled into the slaughterhouse and parked my car. I worked my shift and I thought about it some more as I drove home in silence. And I could barely sleep that night as I thought about it even more while I stared at the ceiling listening to my wife snore as late night turned to early morning.

I'm not sure when I dozed off, but I know I did, and my alarm clock blared, blasting me out of sleep's sweet reprieve. Though I couldn't have slept more than a couple hours, I woke feeling rested. Feeling refreshed. I showered and shaved and ate breakfast and tried my best to ignore my family.

My wife was giving me a bunch of reminders of plans she'd made for me to do this weekend: dinner at her sister's house, trimming the shrubs, and when am I going to get that haircut.

My son and daughter bickered over who got the last bowl of Fruity Pebbles. I'm sure they addressed me with all kinds of questions, but I ignored them all, poured a Thermos of coffee, and got in my truck.

Out of habit more than interest, I flipped the radio on and backed out of the driveway. I hadn't heard anymore about the bomb blast on any other news. I'm usually too exhausted to care about such things when I get home, not to mention I've got to deal with incessant demands from my wife and refereeing the death match that is the rivalry between my two children.

I love them all, at least I think I do, but Christ, when I get home, the last thing I need to hear is kicking and screaming and nagging. Especially over such stupid shit.

If they only knew what a day in my life was like… but they don't, and they don't think that way, and I love them anyway, but sometimes I think that if the lot of them, barking dog included, don't just shut the fuck up, I might murder them in their sleep.

I remembered the tranquility of the silent drive to work yesterday and my hand was on the radio knob, about to kill the sound when the news transitioned to an update on the explosion downtown yesterday. It was a bomb, unfortunately. Could've been terrorists, could've been domestic, could've been some guy with internet access and a grudge. No one knew yet.

I shook my head.

What they did know though was that twenty-two people died and several were severely injured. Most in stable condition, but many lost limbs, and several also lost some of their senses.

Apparently, the bomb blast stole the eyesight, hearing, and smell from a vast majority of the survivors. The news bit ended with the field reporter saying that Memorial Hospital had enough blood to continue, but they were seeking blood donations to replenish their lost supply.

I don't know why this particular explosion worked me the way it did. It was the same thing every week. Israel and Palestine, Afghanistan, dead soldiers, dead civilians, drone strikes, another active shooter, another bomb goes off, a massive apartment fire.

All these atrocities take lives and yet, since they don't affect me directly, I shake my head, but in the end, I don't really give a shit.

This explosion made me give a shit. I thought about the twenty-two dead. I thought about the many more wounded, wondered what it felt like as hot metal and glass cut them to ribbons. As heat singed their hair and melted their skin. What it sounded like as all hell broke loose. I wondered what kind of lives those people had, what their futures were, what their plans were. I wondered what their passions were. And I wondered how many of them had their loved ones and their passions taken from them in a split second.

All of it hit me at once, and I pulled my truck onto the shoulder of the road and switched the radio off. I sat alone with only the sounds of my idling engine, my sobs, and the sounds my fists made as I beat them against the steering wheel.

Tears stung my eyes and snot bubbled from my nose. I wiped it all away with the back of my hand and gripped the wheel, lowered my head, and placed my forehead against it. My agonized war cries turned soft and I just sat there in silence as I thought about all of those poor people. Everything they lost.

Everything the world lost, really. The innocent dead. Sure their families lost a loved one, but what if one of them could've changed this shitty world. Of the twenty-two dead and the several wounded, what about the writer? The artist? The musician? The little league coach? The chef? The funny one? The motivational one?

No one would ever know because the course of their lives had been ended or altered.

I wept harder and I thought about my miserable life and the thing that I hated the most. The thing I hated the most, might salvage this tragedy for at least one person, and if that person was driven, passionate and even a little talented, it might make a point to a whole lot of people.

I didn't go to work. Instead, I turned my truck around and headed to the hospital.

*

"You know, it doesn't really work like this," the doctor said.

"Yeah, well, I don't care. I'm here, and I want to do this. You really gonna get in the way of this?" I answered.

He sighed and shook his head.

"You realize, that you will never, ever hear your grandchildren laugh right?"

"You got any tattoos, doctor?" I asked.

He raised his eyebrows but didn't answer.

"Do you?" I repeated.

"Yes, I do," he said.

"Okay, well you got them because you were passionate about them right? They were the right decision at the time and you didn't care what they'd be like when you got older right?"

"I guess so," he said, "but it's not the same."

"Look," I said, "I love my family, I do, but they never shut up, *ever*. It's constant arguing. And when my kids aren't arguing they are playing music. Do you know what kind of music kids listen to these days? The only words are oh and yeah and baby and there aren't even any fucking instruments."

The doctor laughed and smiled.

"My wife never shuts up, and to be honest doc, I love her, but her voice is not aging well. And she fucking snores."

"But…"

"I'm not finished. Sure, I know what you're going to say, that I still have half my life to go or whatever. Let me tell you doctor, do you know what I do for a living?"

"No, I don't."

"I kill stuff."

"What?"

"I work in a slaughterhouse. All day, it's screaming animals and the 'pffffttt' sound a bolt makes before it punches through a cow's head. I'm that guy. Christ, if I could give you my nose and sense of smell, I'd do that too."

"Jesus," the doctor said.

"Yeah, so I deal with that all day, and my kids don't get it, neither does my wife, they've got their own lives and that's fine, but I drove to and from work yesterday in complete silence and it was the best thing that's ever happened to me. I want to do this. I need to."

"This is highly unorthodox," the doctor said.

"Yeah, well, I'm not here pushing an agenda or something. In fact, I'd like to stay anonymous. I don't want to be on the news or anything. I just want to give something I can no longer stand to someone who's lost what they love. It's really that simple. I don't think many others are coming in here like that, so please, make this happen."

"Alright," the doctor said.

I stood up.

"And make me a promise," I said, "make sure you give them to the person that not only needs them, but the person that will use them."

"I already know who that is. She's got a family and she's got a voice you wouldn't believe. Talent for the piano, too. Her parents told me all about her. Even played a song for me yesterday."

"Good," I said. "Can we do it now?"

He nodded.

*

The doctor took my ears and the organs within them. He gave them to a young woman whose eardrums had burst in the explosion and whose outer ears had fused to the sides of her head. Now she had mine and she could continue playing the piano on nights and weekends and living on the prayer that one day the right person would hear her, and once again, someone would change it all. Having a hell of a story behind her wouldn't hurt either.

My life continued, and I loved it. I no longer had to listen to the screams of the dying animals, the nagging wife, the arguing kids or their shitty music. For the first few months every day was like Christmas.

But I could still read, and my wife bought white boards and dry erase markers for everyone. I didn't have to hear it, but I could sense the hostility in their calligraphy.

The kids still pushed and shoved each other and my wife even went as far as calling me a coward for my sacrifice. She wrote that in big, bold letters. Apparently, and maybe even rightly so, they interpreted my decision as some kind of betrayal.

I put up with it for as long as I could, but they broke me. They needled each other and found new ways to needle me and though the constant silence was comforting, it wasn't enough.

But it did delay the inevitable.

For a little while at least.

I knew how to kill. Been doing it to animals my whole life. And when I finally had enough and used my skills on my family, a family who never knew how to shut the fuck up and appreciate their lives. To be happy that bombs never stole their senses or tore them to pieces…

Well, at least I didn't have to listen to them scream.

ABOUT KERRY G.S. LIPP

Kerry lives in Dayton, Ohio. He hates the sun and loves making fun of dead people. His parents started reading his stories and they've consequently booted him from their will. Kerry's work appears in several anthologies including *DOA2* from Blood Bound Books and *Attack of the B-Movie Monsters* from Grinning Skull Press. His work has been featured multiple times on The Wicked Library podcast. He is currently editing his first novel and shopping a bizarro novella. KGSL rarely (but still) blogs at www. HorrorTree.com and will launch his own website sometime before he dies. Say hi on Twitter @kerrylipp or visit his Facebook page: New World Horror

THE SURPRISE
BY KRISCINDA LEE EVERITT

Referring to her own pregnancy, Lindsay's mother said she knew she'd have twins. Despite the doctor's insistence that there was only one fetus present, she "just knew."

"Because I just wanted you both so badly," she'd say.

Lindsay could see why she herself had gone crazy, but it really started with her now deceased mother.

*

Presently, twenty-seven years later and just three months following her mother's death, Lindsay clicked around the Internet in preparation for her upcoming surgery.

She'd been doing everything she was supposed to do. She practiced her deep breathing, paid special attention to her nutritional intake, and she had laid off anti-inflammatories and blood thinners for over a week now. She stopped eating garlic. She'd even quit smoking a month ago, though she intended to start right back up afterward, once everything was right again.

Again? It's *never* been right.

Right, for the first time in her life.

She clicked the mouse under her right hand.

Her left ear pulled the familiar pull of Lana yawning. It couldn't be heard, for Lana's mouth wasn't connected to Lindsay's larynx or trachea—it would merely go through the motions. Lana was awake.

What time is it?

"It's late," Lindsay answered. "Go back to sleep."

Click: Wikipedia. Click: Edward Mordrake.

What are you doing up?

"Never mind. Can't sleep."

Mordrake, like Lindsay, suffered from *Diprosopus*, otherwise known as "craniofacial duplication." Lana was Lindsay's conjoined twin, though they shared nothing physically. Nothing but the skull over which Lana's features grotesquely spread. Lana had a handful of facial muscles connected wherever they could haphazardly find purchase along Lindsay's cranial ridges, enough to yawn, to smile, to snarl. Lana could not, though, open her eyes. When Lindsay was born, Lana's eyes—plump, but not fully formed—bulged sightless from beneath her lids. It was the only thing about the arrangement that had disturbed their mother, and so, when Lindsay and Lana were two, she'd had them removed.

"If she could see with them, I'd have left them," Lindsay's mother explained.

Are you online?

"Yes," Lindsay answered. "Go back to sleep."

Lana's one ear was functional, though it didn't seem to affect Lindsay's own hearing.

What are you doing? Are you playing a game? You know that keeps me up.

Lindsay couldn't hear Lana, not with her ears, but inside her head. They shared nothing but a skull, and, apparently, some unidentifiable connection inside allowing certain thoughts—Lana's voice—to bridge the synapse-gap between them.

Thankfully, Lindsay thought, not entirely. She'd been allowed to have her own private thoughts.

Mordrake's extra face, like Lana, was voiceless, but he complained bitterly, desperately, that it harangued him at night, "of such things as they only speak of in Hell." He committed suicide at age twenty-three, as no doctor would dare attempt to remove it.

Luckily, Lindsay wasn't living in the 19th century. Lindsay lived in a world of facial transplants, where women who've been doused by their estranged husbands with acid can hope to have a somewhat normal life.

Lana, if she'd had a normal facial bone structure, could be pretty. Maybe. It was hard to tell. But it was better than what that poor woman is dealing with now.

Tomorrow evening, Lindsay would wake up alone for the first time in her life, and that woman—unidentified—would wake up with a new face. Both would awake to new lives.

Where would Lana go?

"Back to Hell," Lindsay said out loud, her finger hovering over the mouse.

What?

"Nothing."

Click, click.

Can't you turn that off and go to sleep? If mom was...

"Mom's dead."

Lindsay shut down her laptop and sat in the dark for a moment, listening to Lana weep quietly until silence finally overtook everything.

*

Where are we going? Something doesn't feel right.

"We're going someplace else today."

Lindsay wore no make up, no nail polish, no perfume, and no jewelry, as per instructions.

Did you request this time off of work? Don't get us fired...

"Us?"

You know what I mean.

"Oh, I know. Don't you worry about anything, Lana. It's all taken care of."

Are we going to the beach?

"When have we ever gone to the beach?"

Never.

"Exactly."

Lindsay put the black Cobalt into *Reverse* and pulled out of her parking space, narrowly missing another early commuter. She slammed the brakes and craned her neck around to look at the driver. It was Mr. Pinion, from two doors down. He glared at her, and she turned her head abruptly to face Lana toward him. Mr. Pinion's tires squealed his escape.

What's going on?

"Mr. Pinion."

What does he want?

"None of this, I assure you."

Lana laughed softly and, for a moment, Lindsay felt guilty.

She could never miss Lana, could she? Maybe. Maybe she could, but not enough to make up for the rest of her life. She was approaching thirty and she'd never had a date. She'd never had a good friend. She'd never been able to walk into a room unnoticed.

Lana wasn't all bad, all the time. She could be demanding, but then, she was hitching a ride on the back of a head that wasn't hers.

So, where are we going? Is it a surprise?

"I'd say so, yes."

Do you remember the surprise parties mom would throw us?

Lindsay did remember. How could she forget? She was the only one present. But their mother instructed her to make sure Lana thought there were streamers and balloons and so many friends, and cake, a big chocolate cake, which Lindsay did without too much trouble. After all, she was used to lying to Lana. Lana lived with parties and friends and even a father who didn't leave on first sight of her. Lindsay, though, had never enjoyed any such luxury.

Lana has never known anything but the sound of Lindsay's voice. What's one more lie?

Is it something like that? Is it our birthday?

"It's someone's birthday."

Whose? Cindy's? Michelle's?

Neither Cindy, nor Michelle, existed.

It's *my* birthday, Lindsay thought.

Whose? Whose? Lana asked giddily.

Lindsay drove to the hospital.

*

From that point, Lindsay stopped communicating with Lana. She parked, entered the hospital, filled out extra forms, changed into a hospital gown, made herself comfortable on the gurney, and waited to be taken into the operating room.

She lay on her back, her face to the side so as not to crush Lana. Lindsay has never laid facing up.

Where are we? This isn't a surprise.

"It is," Lindsay said.

What would happen to Lana? Where would she actually go? Her face would be this poor woman's new face, but where would this voice in Lindsay's head go? It wouldn't stay, would it? It wouldn't go with this unfortunate woman, right? Would Lana just disappear into the ether, like a gas, like a spirit?

What are you thinking?

Lana's voice was flat and low, sending a chill through Lindsay. The room is cold. That's all, Lindsay thought.

What is happening?

Again, Lana's voice droned, shaking, frightened. Lindsay didn't answer.

Lana screamed. Lindsay squinted against it, her hands involuntarily covering her ears, as if it would make a difference. Lana screamed hoarsely, over and over, like a toddler throwing a tantrum.

"You scream all you want, you little bitch," Lindsay yelled back. "Mom's not here and she can't save you!"

Silence. In the room and in Lindsay's head.

Save me?

A nurse peeked her head in.

"Everything okay in here?" she asked, smiling.

"Everything's fine," Lindsay half-smiled. "Bit of a headache."

"You'll be under soon. If it persists after the surgery, we'll see what we can do about it."

"Thank you."

The nurse left.

What. Is. Happening?

"I'll tell you what's happening," Lindsay whispered. "You're out of here. Mom's dead and nothing can keep me from doing this. You're going to be surgically removed and given to someone who actually needs you. Well, not you, but your face. Your up-until-now useless fucking face."

Silence, and then…

Mom won't let you.

"Dead."

Silence.

Cindy won't. Michelle won't let you.

Lindsay paused for a moment, and then thought, what the hell?

"There is no Cindy. No Michelle. I made them up. Mom made me do it. And Dad? He was never there either. He was, but then you came along. We came along. And he left."

You made him leave.

Lindsay reached around and slapped Lana.

You made them all leave.

"Whatever. I'm about to make *you* leave."

You can't.

"Oh, I can. I'm going to. This is it." Lindsay looked at the clock on the wall. "You've got about a half an hour, and then it's bye-bye for little Lana."

Lana said nothing. She said nothing until Lindsay was rolled into the operating room.

Everything was quiet except for the sounds of medicine, centuries of knowledge and technology, squeezed into this comparably tiny room. Edward Mordrake could not have imagined. Neither could his other face, whose name she did not know. Hopefully, no one named it. Lindsay hadn't had a choice.

"Lana and Lindsay, two Ls," their mother sang. "Together, forever, like sisters should be."

Their mother had only ever had brothers.

Something beeped. And again, and repeatedly. Some machine, probably something that would keep her alive during the anesthesia and the thought transformed the beep from something scary to something calming, soothing, almost motherly in its cooing.

Lana hadn't said anything for a long while now, though Lindsay knew she wasn't asleep. When awake, Lana was almost always talking, so this conscious silence was unnerving. But it didn't matter. It was almost time; she was here, now, at the finish line.

Who is this woman?

Lindsay frowned. She'd hoped Lana would stay silent until Lindsay was unconscious. She'd hoped never to hear her voice again. She ignored her sister.

Who is she?

"I don't know. Some woman."

She'll be a better sister than you ever were.

Lindsay found she resented this.

Twenty-seven years of lying to save Lana's feelings, twenty-seven years of following her mother's strict instructions so that Lana could "almost have a normal life," when Lindsay's own life was a constant circus sideshow.

"Lana doesn't need to know about any of that, Lindsay," their mother would say. "Don't you dare say anything to her."

How much better a sister could Lindsay have been?

She'll treat me right.

Lindsay sighed, eyed the clock on the wall. Doctors and nurses now entered the room, gowned and gloved, sterile.

"Hello, Lindsay," a woman's blue-grey eyes appeared, looking down at her from behind a pair of protective goggles that almost looked fashionable. It was Doctor Manvers, the head transplant surgeon. The surgical mask moved with a smile Lindsay couldn't see, but gratefully felt. Only now did she feel afraid, not of Lana, not of what could happen with her, but of the surgery itself.

"Lindsay, this is my assistant, Dr. Treadwell," the doctor said gently. "He'll be helping us today."

Lindsay smiled at them.

I'll bet she lives nearby.

Lindsay's smile faltered.

"Now, let's get you set up," Doctor Treadwell said as Doctor Manvers left to confer with a few of the nurses. "Lindsay, this is Peter, your anesthesiologist. He's a pro; he'll take good care of you."

"Thank you," Lindsay angled her head, still on its side (but not for much longer), up toward the man she couldn't see.

"You're welcome," Peter replied. He sounded nice. "Now, just relax…" He placed a mask over her face.

She'll help me.

"Now, I want you to count backwards from…"

"Help you what?"

"…from ten…"

I'll find you.

"Ten…" Peter began for her.

"You don't know what I look like."

I'll find you.

"Breathe in Lindsay, deeply…nine…"

"No, you won't. You can't."

I will find you.

"…eight…breathe in, Lindsay…"

"How?"

"…seven…six…breathe in…five…"

I'll know your voice.

ABOUT KRISCINDA LEE EVERITT

Kriscinda Lee Everitt is the founder and editor of Despumation Press. She lives in Pittsburgh, Pa with her husband, two cats, and two spooks. She's never had a twin removed, so far as she is aware.

SKINNED
BY MARY PETENSTINE JACKSON

Vincent calls Pepper into his office. He is the head of "The Family" and has been for a very long time. She stops in her tracks and turns to walk in. She notices that the room is tastefully decorated with a heavy oak desk, midnight blue drapes hanging over the curved windows of the turret, and a dark marble floor. She is a little anxious as she enters the room because she has heard some of the gossip going around; gossip about an alliance with the newly formed Dwellers of the Dark. That alliance worries Pepper as she watches Vincent grip the lion head knobs to close the thick doors. He is a pleasant looking man, older and wise, she thinks, as he runs his hand through his dark brown hair. His eyes look sad and concerned and this sets Pepper's nerves even more on edge. She hides the anxiety well with her clear, bright blue eyes and a blank expression on her smooth face. She perches confidently on the office's cream-colored, plush chair.

"He has handpicked you," Vincent informs her.

He is Borok, the High Priest of the Church of Satan and the figurehead of the Dwellers of the Dark.

She shifts slightly in her chair, wanting to run and hide. Being picked by him for anything was never good. Vincent walks towards her and places a fatherly hand on her shoulder.

In a shaky voice, he explains Borok's selection. "He wants your fair, white skin."

A small shudder travels through her.

"There isn't much time before the Necromancer and others from the church come to take you."

She knows there will be five other members of the church and she knows exactly where they will take her, into the lowest of the catacombs beneath the castle.

He continues, "You know this is of the utmost importance to our clan. I won't lie… it will be extremely painful and very uncomfortable for quite some time after the procedure, but you must offer yourself to this."

Pepper hangs her head slightly, "Yes sir, I understand."

"This isn't only to solidify The Family's alliance with the Dwellers of the Dark, it will also ensure that we will stand together when the Hierarchy crumbles."

A moment later, they hear a knock on one of the big doors. Vincent crosses the room and opens the door a crack. Pepper tries to make out what is being said, but hears only urgent tones and mumbled, rushed speech. Seconds after closing the door, Vincent hands her a white cotton gown.

"Change, quickly!"

He leaves her alone in the room where she changes and waits.

When Vincent returns, he offers to walk her to the tunnel opening of the catacombs. She accepts and turns toward the doors, but is surprised when Vincent heads to the fireplace. *A secret passage*, she thinks as they walk in silence. Teeth chattering, Pepper shivers, unsure of whether it's the dark, dank passageway or the fear building in her. Her mind turns to what she knows of the age-old torture and means of punishment, being flayed alive. They will start on either her arm or leg, and work their way around until all of her skin is removed. She thinks of what will happen to her.

Someone approaches the small group from behind, but Pepper is too deep in thought to care. She feels a pinch as something punctures the back of her neck. Her knees go weak and she experiences a falling sensation as everything goes black.

As Pepper awakes, she is completely immobile, save only slight movement of her head. Her body is in a never-ending, open jumping jack pose, both ankles and wrists being pulled to their limits, fastened to short chains. A slight breeze cools her head, which she realizes is now clean-shaven.

She tries to lift her chin and looks around the cavern surrounding her. Lit candles bathe her in a circle of light, rendering her unable to make out any features of the large group of hooded figures standing in the shadows. Off to the far right, Borok stands before a podium, holding a book. Chanting, he picks it up and waves it in the air. As he approaches her, Pepper's eyes widen.

On the spine of the book, fine hairs and freckles dot the surface. The cover is pale and soft. She can see what looks like a birthmark or a mole on the back cover.

Skin, she thinks. *The book is made of skin! Is this how mine will be used?*

A mammoth of a man leads a group of four other men in from the left, each holding a more menacing flaying tool than the one before him: a four-inch flat-top blade with a curved hook on the top edge, a tree purser-looking tool with a short handle, a saw with wicked teeth, and the last one, a six-inch blade on one side and a ripper on the back part at the top. The four men surround Pepper, two flanking her sides, one at her head, and one at her toes. Her thoughts are racing and she wants to scream out for someone to help her.

But she has been chosen and therefore, she shouldn't complain. She must sacrifice her temporary comfort for the good of her people.

The height of her fear makes her feel faint and extremely aware at the same time. Borok continues to chant in an obscure tongue, completely unintelligible to Pepper.

Suddenly, the mass of hooded figures chants back to their High Priest. With a wave of his hand, the four men simultaneously commence their cutting. Long, ear splitting screams of agony let loose from Pepper's throat as tears begin to break free. The tools pierce her skin and the fat layer beneath. The blood trickles to the floor with each cut, slash, and pull of her skin. Her body begins to convulse from the pain. The candlelight seems to dim and the sounds drift far away as the trauma sends her into shock.

When Pepper comes to again, she cannot make sense of what she is feeling, seeing or hearing. She feels groggy, as if she has been under for hours, and she cannot move or scream, even though white-hot pain threatens to send her mind back into the dark. As the fogginess in her brain starts to clear, she feels wet and sticky.

Why am I in such unbearable pain? Where am I?

A figure jogs Pepper's memory and she tries to remember. *Boobrick? Burocks? No, not right...Borok! Oh my god!* Sweeping, seeping blood and fluid ooze out from where skin once was. A horrified gasp escapes her parched throat as realization and panic set in.

How long does it take for a vampire to regenerate a full body of skin? She feels a hard tug and sharp pain as her epidermis slides to the floor with a wet, smacking sound. Darkness envelops her again.

Jarring pain brings her back, eyes wide open, as she bounces on the cold floor, the searing, burning feeling on her heels triggering her senses to high alert. She feels rough, moist hands binding her wrists, pulling and stretching her arms as she tries to focus. Something runs down her face. Through her haze, she can see smears, drips and drag marks trailing behind her on the stone.

An iron gate opens with a long squeak. Borok's voice drones on and on, chanting words that have no meaning to Pepper. "That is not dead, which can eternal lie! With the strange eons, even death may die! That is not dead, which can eternal lie! With the strange eons, even death may die!"

Light temporarily blinds her as she is dragged into a dazzling ceremonial chamber. She is crudely thrown against a wall, pain continuing to needle her body.

Pepper turns towards Borok's voice and sees two robed men fitting her pale, blood smeared skin over what looks like a badly decayed, broken body. Her stomach pitches and rolls, and she lets out a blood-curdling scream of anger, pain, horror and grief as the darkness closes in on her yet again, even without eyelids.

This time, she awakens in her own plush and lavish bedchamber. If not for the pain and intravenous tubes snaking through the gauze wrapped around her body, she would have written the experience off as a horrible nightmare. She hears a sweet, soft whisper. She knows that voice…it's her friend, Lydia. A small smile creeps across her face, causing her to wince. Lydia is a petite, dark-haired, cheery lady. She offers Pepper a sip of water.

Lydia is known to prattle on when she is nervous or angry, and right now she is both. *Vincent was so wrong to do this to Pepper!* she thinks.

"Why do the Dwellers of the Dark need so many organs and tissues from us vampires for the demons they raise anyway? I think Borok just gets a kick out of torturing our kind. Thank goodness you *aren't* human, Pepper, or you would have died within a few hours of the start of your ordeal. As it is, you've been incoherent for a week! I've been beside you the whole time – you never came to but you have moaned and whimpered a bit so I assumed you were having a terrible dream."

She had been.

*

Walking the halls of the large castle, it seemed too quiet.

"Hello," Pepper called out to no one in particular. "Where is everyone?"

She heard a close, rumbling growl and strained to see by the light of the chamber stick in her still bandaged hand. The growl became closer still. She turned to see a pair of glowing red eyes and froze in mid-step. A voice in her head then yelled at her to RUN AND RUN FAST! Danger is approaching!

Her candle suddenly revealed one of the most disgusting and disturbing sights she had ever seen. Deep within her she somehow knew…this was the demon who was the recipient of her skin, donated only a few months ago. It was larger than a man, gray in color, with black and brown spike-like, bony partitions sticking out from the gaps. A greenish-red pus-looking substance seeped from tiny holes where skin was stitched onto the corpse's frame. What an abomination of her formerly beautiful, smooth, white skin!

The demon lunged forward, its huge, sharp, meat hook claws reaching out for her; its grotesque mouth opening wide. The last thing Pepper saw were three rows of dagger-like teeth as she fell back in fear, limb by limb being torn from her body.

*

Pepper, dehydrated, manages a single tear down her cheek. The nightmare was horrifying and she is thankful to have such a caring and dedicated friend by her side. In painful time, her body would repair itself, but would her mind?

Forever is a *very* long time.

ABOUT MARY PETENSTINE JACKSON

Mary has been writing since she was in elementary school. She has penned short stories and articles for P.E.T.S. Magazine, entered writing competitions and won a few times, as well as written a family history book filled with funny stories. She considers herself "a jack of all trades, but the master of none." When she is not writing she enjoys: repurposing old items into something new, crafting, deep woods camping & hiking, swimming, reading, gardening, music, singing, playing with her grandkids and spending time with family. She has a wicked sense of humor and loves all things darker or horror related.

THE CLARINET
BY MEGAN LEE BEALS

Golden Voice Virginia Hart was not an organ donor but when she saw the pictures of the crash and her daughter's hamburger throat, she knew she had to give. And now she watched the girl rattle breathing through slick, white machines and a mountain of gauze that disguised the puncture of glass through her neck that almost severed the spine. Another centimeter would have paralyzed her, and anything after that would have been death. The doctors pieced her sweet little Vee back together and again Virginia cycled through the bloody pictures knowing that the voice she worked so hard to build out of the stubborn girl was lost forever. But every day the voice changes, something lost from days before and something gained as well, though what Golden Voice Virginia gained with age did not help sell her records.

She hunted down the surgeon assigned to her daughter and when he refused she found another to fix her daughter's voice. An electronic prosthesis could not take the place of the strong, beautiful cords Virginia built up through seventeen difficult years. Vee would receive an implanted vocal cord, donated by her mother, and the golden voice would train itself to use a single vocal cord, one reed to flutter against a synthetic membrane lodged inside the larynx.

"We'll be two clarinets in a world full of oboes, Vee," she whispered to the black and blue girl, singing words *dolcissimo* near the puffy, shovel face that had always looked more like her mistake of a father. A shame the surgeon would only work on her throat.

"We'll make a comeback," said Virginia in a hospital gown

as the nurses strapped her down onto the bed beside her daughter.

Virginia's reed was white, the muscle pink, and when the surgeon took it living from her he replaced the treasured thing with a membrane of Virginia's own design. The surgeon insisted it needn't be fancy; the membrane was only to close a gap, to keep the air from moving past without consent of the single cord and Virginia blushed and fanned her face when she told her surgeon of the filament she'd like inlaid in the white membrane. Her sacrifice should be marked in gold.

"But don't you tell a soul," she said because the vanity was almost too shameful and it would sell better as a rumor.

When she woke the surgeon told her to scream.

"I've never screamed in my life," breathed husky, broken-voiced Virginia, but she had to write it out on a whiteboard before the surgeon understood what she tried to say.

"Screaming will build your muscle. It has to compensate for its other half."

"My daughter," mouthed Virginia, reminded of her missing half, but the girl could not go home with her. Vee's injuries were still too severe, the throat under construction. The girl needed another week and on her way out of the hospital, Virginia took a dry erase pen and scrawled across the white board in Vee's room "DO NOT SCREAM."

She wrote it again in the white shadow of erased letters every day she came to visit.

Virginia would not damage her remaining vocal cord with screaming. She built the muscle through diligent practice, running *allegretto* through her scales, higher and higher to reclaim her register, and recorded the progress to ensure not a day passed without improvement. In a moment of pride, Virginia let a practice leak on the internet to coincide with a third page story of a famous singer sacrificing her vocal cord to let her daughter sing again. Her voice had taken on a shimmery quality, so steady and strong that it couldn't be human. Letters trickled into her mailbox, offers to duet with artists on stadium circuits, to feature in videos, to sing for places that had forgotten her, and in the rush her daughter disappeared.

"Where is she?" *Con forza!* Roaring at the orderlies was as close as Virginia ever got to screaming.

Vee's father checked her out of the hospital, drifting bastard who only cared for the girl when it would upset Virginia Hart. She called through every number she could remember attached to the man and when that yielded naught, she dropped in on the bastard's mother and pounded on the door.

"Is she screaming?" she asked the woman who couldn't be bothered to keep track of her own damned son. "If Vee took that doctor's advice over her own mother's I'll..." But the woman only watched dumbfounded and Virginia left through the open door without finishing her threat. A handsome young pianist would meet her in an hour and anger upsets the voice.

Vee had run away before, always to come back just as soon as the old bastard remembered how much he hated being a father. And then the training would begin. Virginia would build up her own muscle inside the girl's larynx; two clarinets, and a single voice that could live twice. The girl would be a commodity when she was gone, a living ghost of her mother's golden voice. And titters of literal gold in Virginia Hart's throat spread across the internet.

*

She sang for the pianist, and for the opera and for everyone for a month while her records sold into second and third pressings and then one day her daughter knocked against her door.

"Sweetheart?" asked Virginia and she looked past the girl, but saw no sign of her father.

Vee stepped into the house and hugged her mother, then pulled away and mouthed the word "Mom" because she had no sound to put behind it.

"Have you been screaming?"

Vee nodded. The whole month she'd been screaming, finding an embryonic voice in that cadenza of scars across her neck like a mangled recapitulation of the long attractive cut worn proudly across her mother's throat.

"You're abusing the gifts I've given you," said Virginia as if a gift still belonged to its giver, but Vee knew to rough a gift, file down its serial numbers, take away its pretty, inorganic sheen and make it something real.

She took her mother's slender hand and steadied that busted cord just enough to whisper out in a coal-dark voice that belonged to no one yet: "Yes mom. I am."

The golden voice hummed *dolente*, a tuneless note that spoke of irredeemable loss for its other half, and the woman attached could not understand that her daughter never meant to sing.

ABOUT MEGAN LEE BEALS

Megan Lee Beals lives in Tacoma, Washington with her husband and a one eyed cat. Her fiction has been featured online at Literary Orphans and Luna Station Quarterly, and anthologized in Stamps Vamps & Tramps and The Future Embodied. When not writing or knitting or collecting hobbies, Megan works in a bookstore where she enjoys an unconventional and ongoing education in fiction (unaccredited).

SUM OF MY PARTS
BY RIVKA JACOBS

As usual, I felt uncomfortable.

"You're still repressing conflicting emotions," my biomedical team leader, Dr. Hennessy, said. I followed him and the nurse down the antiseptic, green and white corridor. "It's important for you to see exactly what the process looks like," he added without turning around.

We stopped in front of the lab door. Well, *my* lab door—the entire ten-story building is a massive lab complex and this is my special section of the whole. As we passed single file into the room, the soft fluorescent panels above ticked on. I entered last, paused, steadied myself, took several deep breaths. The place smelled like astringent, the surfaces sterile, shiny, cold; I was glad I remembered to wear a jacket. I watched my shoes. I heard Dr. Hennessy click something on a keyboard; there was a moment of electric silence but I knew what he was doing, sweeping his fingers back and forth over a control screen like a virtuoso pianist playing a sonata.

"Mr. Melwani, we're ready," the nurse gently said, from right next to me. I might have grimaced, or given some twist to my mouth—I didn't mean to—and I could hear the doctor clear his throat.

Okay, okay, look up, look at it, no one else seems to have these problems, I said to myself. I raised my eyes.

It was awake. Or rather, I was awake. Or my facsimile was awake—the partial mannequin, the three-dimensional collagen-matrix mesh bent to human shape upon which was hung the bioengineered parts I would need as I aged or got sick or injured.

I would have preferred my bioficial organs kept in Pyrex cylinders, floating in nutrient baths. But Dr. Hennessy explained to me years ago—the human body remained a discreet organism, even when separated into pieces. Scientists discovered that the system, the complete interrelated, interdependent biological system was the best way to keep the anatomical elements healthy and ready.

I stared at him, *it*, the collection, the sum of my parts. It was standing casually, life-sized, in a ventilated germ-free, safety-glass bioenclosure that looked more like a cage. The thing always made my stomach tighten, my chest spasm with anxiety. I gazed into the two brown irises, through crystal clear corneas. I saw the white balls of its eyes, my eyes, bioassembled copies of my eyes derived from my own cells. Half the face was covered with a fine mat of skin. The lax mouth was all red muscle with a glimpse of pearly teeth. The skull was open at the top, a brain growing inside. The lungs puffed and flattened, the heart—the deep, deep red, almost purple heart was beating. All the major organs were there, pulsing and twitching with life, in case I would need them.

"Your pancreas and kidneys are back," Dr. Hennessy said, standing in his white lab-coat, his arms folded across his chest. He was smiling. "See?"

I wanted to leave. "I'm grateful," I answered stupidly. My Type II diabetes had been cured with a new pancreas, and both kidneys, complete with new adrenal glands. I stared at the lower legs—veins and arteries, tibia and fibula, tendons and long muscles, suspended in place, living, feeding, giving off waste. I glanced up once more at the face. I thought the eyes moved, focusing on me as I stepped closer. "It sees me," I said. "It knows I'm here."

Dr. Hennessy sighed, straightened, checked his watch. "Well, Mr. Melwani ... come closer, you shouldn't be so squeamish ... here, let me show you; we'll be replacing your aortic arch, the ascending and descending aorta. The tear you have is tiny, but it can cause an aneurysm at any time."

I only half heard him go on about my aging, sclerotic, inelastic arteries; I was studying my other, that montage of me.

Its heart seemed to pump more quickly. The yellowish pleura, the blue-gray lungs expanded, contracted, the diaphragm lifting and falling with greater urgency. I could see skin swatches rippling, every visible muscle fiber tensed. Fight or flight? Some autonomic nervous system response? "Can this hear you?" I asked the doctor. I pointed, tried to sound as if I was making light of the situation, "It's like he heard you and knows you'll be taking his aorta, which kind of means this incarnation of him, of me, is going to die...."

Dr. Hennessy did not appear amused. "'It can't die. It isn't a person. And we provide continuity, continual regeneration. Look, there ... turn your head ... no not you, him...."

And it did, it shifted its head on that pivot joint between the first and second cervical vertebra.

"There, that's a fully formed ear. All the working parts, in case you need them, which you will as you get older and older."

It stayed like that, skull-muscles-cartilage-nerves-flesh-teeth averted, heart thudding, lungs ballooning up and collapsing. Like it was having a panic attack. Like me.

Exactly like me.

ABOUT RIVKA JACOBS

Rivka Jacobs and currently lives with two Siamese cats in West Virginia, but was born in Philadelphia and grew up in South Florida. She has a BA in history, MAs in sociology and mental health counseling, and a BSN. She recently worked as a psychiatric nurse. Rivka has one grown son, a pharmacist, who lives in Philadelphia.

ERASER
BY STEPHEN D. ROGERS

Natasha plucked one of his chest hairs.

"Ouch!" Greg couldn't remember how many drinks he'd had last night; could really only remember the one. After all, she paid him to perform.

"Have you ever wondered why men have nipples?"

"I never really thought about it." He shifted his head on the pillow to better see her face. "I hope that doesn't come as too much of a disappointment to you."

"No, but then I expect so little." She grinned up at him. "I would no more turn to you for satisfying conversation than I would to a screen for great sex."

Greg entwined his fingers behind his head and smiled. He'd learned long ago to take the compliments where he could find them. "Are you in the mood for more of that great sex?"

"Not right now." Natasha traced circles on his chest. "I'm more interested in your body."

Whatever that meant. Greg almost said her fingernail felt good on him, but didn't.

The sharp red looked good against his tanned skin, but he couldn't really feel it. Maybe just the slightest tingle.

"Do you have any plans for us today?"

"Oh, we'll think of something." Natasha hummed as she drew spirals on him.

Greg closed his eyes and concentrated on the sensations of Natasha's nearness. The minty smell of her hair. The warmth of her flesh. The weight of her leg on his.

But he couldn't really feel that finger.

She stopped humming. "Do you remember pencils?"

"Sure. They still made them when I was in kindergarten. They were yellow."

"The mass produced ones, yes. But there were also smaller batches of mass produced ones painted in different colors." Natasha sighed. "I always loved to draw, to take a blank sheet of paper and create something out of nothing, just me and my pencil."

"I thought you had an artistic sensibility."

Natasha laughed. "I'm sorry. It's just that sometimes you surprise me."

Assume she meant that as a compliment and move on. "Look at how you've decorated this room. You can't even buy most of this stuff any longer."

"My favorite things are the items I made myself. That lamp on the other side of the bed. The wooden candlestick on the dresser. My walking stick."

"You're very talented."

"The most difficult part in making my own pencils is inserting the shaft of graphite and clay down the hole."

"Yeah, that sounds difficult."

Natasha chuckled. "Actually, it's simple. It's two pieces of wood glued together around the shaft."

"Oh. Still, it's impressive you can make a pencil."

"That's right, you don't make anything, do you?" Natasha pouted. Nodded. "Women create, and men destroy. If history has taught us nothing else, it has taught us that. Still, you can contribute."

"Whatever I can do to help, you know I'm here for you. Whatever you waa. Waa." His mouth had stopped working properly. "Waaeva."

She pinched him.

He saw her do it, but didn't feel a thing. Tried to move, but couldn't.

Natasha smiled. "I'm so glad you agree. As a matter of fact,

the most difficult part of making a pencil is finding a good eraser."
    She tweaked his right nipple.
    "Oh, look."

ABOUT STEPHEN D. ROGERS

Stephen D. Rogers is the author of *Shot to Death*, *Three-Minute Mysteries*, and more than 900 shorter works. His website, www. StephenDRogers.com, includes a list of new and upcoming titles as well as other timely information.

DONORS TO THE STARS
BY JORDAN PHELPS

Mr. Coleman was watching the evening news when the doorbell rang. At first he ignored it, but when the second ring came he slammed the footrest of his La-Z-Boy down and reached for his cane. If they cared enough to ring twice, a third would almost certainly follow. Mr. Coleman walked down the hallway, muttering "at this hour?" as if six o'clock was an absurd time for a visit, then he pulled the door open and looked down at the young girl standing on his porch. Her hair was done up in blond pigtails and she held a cardboard UNICEF collection box. She was proudly rattling the change inside.

"Hi, Mister," she said, flashing him a genuine smile. "I'm collecting money to give to the kids who can't afford the things we can. Have any change? It's for school." She held out the box, gazing up at him hopefully.

"Not today," said Mr. Coleman.

"Oh, well I can come back tomor-"

Mr. Coleman shut the door before she had time to finish. He walked back to his La-Z-Boy, muttering about how pushy kids were these days, and then turned his attention back to the news. The reporter spoke gravely about a shooting that had left one dead and two injured, and then carried on in the same tone to discuss the rising cost of gasoline. The shooting captured Mr. Coleman's interest, but as the stories decreased in shock value he began to nod off. Soon he was asleep, and the reporter's voice was no longer a message, but a hollow noise drifting through empty halls.

*

Jack coughed a mouthful of smoke into the night air and then thrust the joint towards Brandon. "Man, don't be such a puss. Just take one drag. You'll love it."

"What if we get caught?" asked Brandon.

"It's almost midnight. Who's gonna catch us?"

Brandon looked around the park and saw nothing but shadows, trees, and rusty play equipment. "Nobody, I guess." He took the joint from between Jack's thumb and index finger, and, for a while, just stared at it, shivering in the cool breeze.

"Put it to your mouth and inhale," said Jack.

Brandon bit his lip. Maybe if he took off his shirt before he smoked his parents wouldn't be able to smell it on him. He reached for his collar, but then decided it was a stupid idea and lowered his arm again. They'd probably already be able to smell it on him anyway. He was about to hand the joint over to Jack when he heard a faint buzzing noise that slowly began to grow like an approaching swarm of bees.

"You hear that?" asked Jack.

Brandon nodded.

"Well, what the hell is it?" Jack wanted to know, but Brandon could no longer hear him. The buzzing had grown louder, closer, almost as if it were coming from inside their heads. Jack looked around frantically, saw nothing and then turned his head up to the stars. They seemed to be moving, shaking against each other and dancing in strange formations. He thought he was going to pass out. But, as he teetered between consciousness and what lay beyond, the buzzing began to retreat, and the stars returned to their respective positions in the sky. Jack blinked a couple times, as if to confirm that the stillness he now saw was indeed reality.

Without thinking, Brandon put the joint to his lips and took a long pull. Then he coughed out the smoke and took another.

"Shit, man. Give me that." Jack held out a shaky arm and snatched the joint from Brandon, putting it immediately to his mouth.

They remained silent for a long time, passing the joint back and forth and looking up to the stars every couple minutes to make sure they were still where they should be.

*

Mr. Coleman was jolted awake by a shrill noise, but it was gone before he could open his eyes to search for the source, leaving only the faint drone of the television. He scratched his head and looked around the living room, but saw nothing. Maybe he had just imagined it. His watch displayed the time 12:00 in glaring red digits, as if it were scolding him for nodding off in the evening again. Mr. Coleman sighed. He sat up in his chair, picked up the television remote and began flipping through channels, hoping to find something that would put him back to sleep.

He passed over the late shows with Letterman and Leno and then hovered on a soft-core Latino porno for a couple minutes before moving reluctantly on. The next channel played an infomercial. The salesman's hands moved tenderly over the wallet he was trying to sell, which was clearly better than other wallets, he explained, because the card pockets were larger and the leather was finer. The words *call now* appeared in giant text, followed by a toll-free number. Mr. Coleman laughed, doubting everything the man said, but at the same time his hand began to creep from the chair towards the telephone. He tried to pull it away, but found he had no control over it. Now he was dialing the toll-free number. A sales representative would be on the other end at any moment, ready to accept his credit information. Mr. Coleman already had a wallet. Why should he need this one? He tried to hang up before the other voice came on to greet him, but still, he couldn't do it. Something was stopping him. What the hell was it?

Now the sales representative was on the line, building up the product. But none of that mattered to Mr. Coleman. He cut her off and said he wanted to place an order, which was fine by her. And now he was reading off the numbers on his credit card that he had just removed from his perfectly good, current wallet.

With the order placed and the phone returned, Mr. Coleman

was left confusedly staring at the television screen and trying to make sense out of what had just happened, but there was no sense to make of it. He continued watching the same infomercial until he nodded off, afraid of what the next channel might convince him to do if he dare change it.

*

The next day, businesses thrived in the town of Kingsville. Candies and toys were plucked from shelves by confused parents who, having initially dismissed their children's requests, found their hands to be sailing through the air independent of thought, and with the sole purpose of transferring merchandise into carts. Children screamed, hands reacted, and business owners smiled, watching over their stores in a state of dazed, near dream-like euphoria.

Chores were completed before noon and without argument, leaving houses cleaner than they ever had been, especially the rooms of children. They had lined up their toys neatly on dressers and bookshelves and played with only one at a time – something most of them had never done in their lives.

Even the air felt different in Kingsville now, as if the particles were moving about in new, mysteriously choreographed patterns.

*

Brandon and Jack were just waking up now at half past noon. Last night, following their strange encounter, they had returned to Brandon's basement where they watched a marathon of comedies. Neither of them laughed; they simply stared at the screen—grateful for its sounds and images—while they tried to determine independently what could have caused the buzzing and the shifting of stars. Eventually they had both fallen asleep, leaving the final comedy to play out until it gave way to the darkness and silence they had been avoiding.

*

Nicole skipped down the street towards home, wishing the school had provided her with a larger UNICEF collection box. It was hardly even lunchtime and she had filled the entire thing, which made her happy—especially for the children that needed the money—but she really did miss the clinking noise the coins made when there had been room for them to collide. No matter—she'd empty the box at home and be out collecting donations again by one.

After this morning's haul Nicole was actually beginning to believe that she could win the grand prize offered to the student who collected the most donations: a four kilogram, dairy milk chocolate bar. Just the thought of it caused her to smile and salivate. And that's exactly what she was doing when the giant shadow of a mechanical hulk covered her completely, sucking the light and warmth from the day like spilled sugar into a vacuum. It soared recklessly over her head, coughing and sputtering like an army of dying motorcycles and soaring past streets and houses before eventually landing on an empty soccer field in the park.

Nicole forgot all about the four kilogram chocolate bar and began running towards the soccer field. At first she thought the thing was an airplane, but as she neared her destination she realized it was much more conical, and had landed upright with its nose facing the clouds – like a metallic party hat, she thought. As she watched, a hatch opened up in the side of the craft and several men hopped out of it, scrambling to erect a red and white tent that reminded Nicole of the circus.

Her curiosity intensified as she was able to see more of what was happening ahead, and by the time she arrived the tent was up and one of the men stood patiently in front of it, as if time didn't matter to him in the slightest. A sign hung above the tent's entrance that read: *Donations. Please form a line and advance when you are able to.*

"Hello," the man said simply. "Thank you for volunteering. You are the first. Please, come with me." The man motioned towards the tent's opening with his arms and then walked through it, clearly expecting her to follow him inside.

But Nicole didn't want to. She was undeniably curious, but

what was all this about volunteering to donate? And where had these men even come from? The more she thought about it, the more she wanted to turn around and go home. But somehow she couldn't. It was as if her shoes were glued to the ground. And now they began to move themselves clumsily up and down in a half shuffle, bringing her to the tent's entrance. Nicole fought with her body, commanding it to turn around, but it continued forward, robot-like and without hesitation until she was inside.

Including the man that had coaxed her in, there were three of them inside, all standing next to an operating table. An assortment of chrome machinery lined the tent and reflected the intense lighting from the fixtures that had been attached to the roof. How they had put all of this together in less than a minute, Nicole would never know. But right now it wasn't her greatest concern.

"Please step onto the table and assume the fetal position," said the man from outside.

Nicole couldn't remember what the fetal position was exactly. She knew she had heard about it at some point, but before could ask for a refresher, her body had stepped onto the table and assumed the position.

"Good. Now we are going to anesthetize you. Please remain still." The man brought out a needle and walked around to the other side of the table.

Until this point, the men had looked completely human, but now, as their smiles grew into perverse grins, they looked anything *but* human. Their mouths seemed almost triangular, with teeth that were long and thin like shards of clear glass; their limbs elongated and flowed through the air like thin, helium balloons; they watched Nicole with wide, intelligent eyes that seemed to be grinning with a madness she couldn't even begin to understand.

Nicole felt a sharp sting as the needle slid into her lower back. The last thing she saw before closing her eyes was a large vat at the back of the tent labeled *Cerebrospinal Fluid*.

*

Over the next hour, the entire population of Kingsville migrated towards the tent as if attracted by some primal call elusive to the five major senses. People joined the line without much thought–adhering to the pleasant buzz of curiosity that had lifted them from their homes–and there was hardly any talk of what might be happening, at least, not until they reached the sign above the tent. And by then it was much too late to turn back.

*

Mr. Coleman was almost at the front of the line when he saw the unconscious body of a teenage girl collapse head first onto the grass around the back corner of the tent. Only the top half of her body was visible, but it was soon dragged behind the tent once more.

He tried to run, finding himself unable to move his body. And when the line advanced, so did he, as if a strong current was pulling him closer and closer to the tent. Soon he felt the sting of the needle as well.

*

The sky grew dark as the line continued to shuffle towards the tent, and it was almost midnight when the last *volunteer* stepped inside. Now, with their vat full of fluid, the humanoid beings wheeled it over to the mechanical hulk they had rode in on and attached it to the base, causing the entire craft to buzz with energy. They brought down the red and white tent as quickly as they had put it up–all of the complex machinery disappearing into its many folds–and then they too entered the craft, which immediately rose into the night sky and disappeared into the stars.

*

Brandon was the first one to shrug off unconsciousness the next morning, and he found himself standing over a sea of sleeping bodies that covered the entire field. Each of them was facing the sky and laying so still that for a moment he thought they were corpses.

Slowly now, people began to rise up from all over the crowd as if summoned by the sun's awakening. They stretched, looked around confusedly, and then most of them walked off towards their homes, rubbing their temples. The few that stayed complained about the terrible headaches they were feeling, and tried to piece together what must have happened the previous night for the whole town to end up asleep in the park; strange hypotheses were stated – as they always are in times of mysterious uncertainty – but the consensus was clear: *nobody* had a damn clue.

So the people did what came naturally to them; they shuffled back to their houses and offices where everything made sense, and even the most challenging questions had answers if they just searched hard enough for them. Their headaches faded as they settled back into their normal lives, but after that night, not a single resident of Kingsville could gaze up at the stars without feeling an impetuous sense of dread.

ABOUT JORDAN PHELPS

Jordan Phelps has had fiction published in various anthologies, including Dead Harvest, Return to Deathlehem: An Anthology of Holiday Horrors for Charity, and A Chimerical World: Tales of The Seelie Court. He lives in Ontario where he spends much of his time recording daydreams and watching bees open doors.

THE SAVIOR
BY K.A. MORRIS

It started innocently enough, as these things most often do, with a blood drive at a local church. After filling out the requisite paperwork, he sat with countless others to donate a bit of himself to help save the life of another. A few vials of blood, a wink and a nod to the nurse that had taken his samples—a quick exchange with another attendant for an oatmeal cookie and a glass of juice, and he was ready to be on his way. Nothing out of the ordinary here. Except that, while munching his dry cookie on his way out the door, he was stopped by a supervisor in a neat, grey uniform with tired lines on her face. He had a unique blood type, she explained, and would he consider donating more blood? Coming into the clinic later that week? Hesitant, he said he would consider it; he had a busy week coming up and a conference to prepare for. He took the card for the clinic politely, but thinking to himself that it wasn't necessary, he'd done his civic duty already, after all. His week continued in a mindless corporate whirl, greys, browns, shades of life that didn't fully register, but happened all the same without complaint or too much fuss. That was his life, passing by in muted tones. But that was all about to change.

*

Weeks had passed since his trip to the blood drive. It was another beige-colored Tuesday, a thermos of coffee beside him as he made notes in his ledger. Accounting was his life. It was orderly, predictable; it paid the bills, and kept his wife at home where she expected to be in this day and age. She could have worked, but he knew that she enjoyed the ordinary duties of housewifery while her friends went to typing pools and fretted about finding a good husband so they wouldn't have to take dictation or answer phones anymore. That was the secret about "women's lib" they didn't *really* want to be equal, they just wanted to talk about it over cocktails while their husbands did the dishes. His life was just the way he liked it. Calm. And like accounting, orderly and utterly predictable. A voice came over the loudspeaker—a call for him. Unusual. No one ever called the office for him. Not even his wife. He didn't even get mail at the office. He carefully marked his place in the ledger, closed and straightened it on the desk. Walking to the common phone, he lifted the goldenrod yellow receiver to his ear and pressed the flashing red line button. On the other end of the line, was the blood donation clinic. There had been a terrible accident, one of the victims matched his blood type—oh yes, very rare, and there was something very special about his blood too, antibodies found nowhere else—and could he consider coming in at once? It was a matter of life and death. He nodded into the phone; of course he would come directly.

Confirming the address, he cradled the phone, and walked briskly to his desk. Having never left the office other than at the exact time he was supposed to for the past eight years, the receptionist was stunned to see him leave. He offered no explanation, it was life or death—and he had to go. It was more than his civic duty; it was now a calling, a higher purpose. Grey, brown, beige—the colors whirled past the windows of the bus as he made his way to the clinic.

The donation went smoothly, he gave as much as they would let him. Sipping orange juice and talking easily with the nurse, she explained to him how important his donation was, that he was saving a precious life, how unique his blood was. He nodded magnanimously—it was the least he could do, the very least, and would they keep him informed of how the patient was after the transfusion was complete? It was oddly important to him to know that his precious donation wasn't going to waste. As he left the clinic, he made sure to remind the grey uniformed supervisor again that he was very interested in the outcome of his donation, to ensure that it was given to the correct person, that he hadn't left the office for nothing on that beige Tuesday afternoon. He also gave strict instruction, perhaps making it a little more strict than intended, that his donation was to be kept anonymous. The rest of his evening passed as they usually did, meatloaf, small talk over dinner, a glass of whiskey, and then to bed to stare at the streetlights on the ceiling while his wife snored beside him. He hadn't mentioned anything to her about the donation, and he wouldn't, she knew very little about his life, and this was his special little secret. That night, when he did eventually dream, instead of black and white, he dreamed in shades of red.

*

The next day as he read the morning paper waiting for the city bus to take him to another navy blue colored Wednesday in the financial district, a story caught his eye that he would normally have skimmed over. A miraculous, life saving transfusion had brought a prominent local politician back from the brink of death. The unknown donor with the golden blood was lauded as an angel in disguise, the likes of which the city had never seen. He chuckled to himself, cheeks warming at the private pleasure he took from this. *His* blood had done this, *His* selfless act. The rest of his day passed as they usually did, orderly, predictably. But on this particular navy blue Wednesday, his hands trembled ever so slightly as they wrote endless numbers in the ledger. He re-read the newspaper article several times that day, countless times, a private smile on his lips. Each time feeling that heat inside—that private pleasure that *He* had done this wonderful thing. That *He* had given life. The bus ride at the end of the day passed more quickly than usual, he missed his stop and had to backtrack—in eight years that had never happened.

That night, after his usual glass of whiskey, he did not go to bed. Instead, he went to his study, a small room neatly filled with leather-bound books on various mundane subjects, with a wooden desk on which sat a partially finished ship model that he worked on during weekends. Nursing his drink, he pushed aside the schooner he was building, carefully clipped the article about his donation from the newspaper, and slid it into the middle drawer of the desk. Moving the model back to its proper place on the desk, he twisted the ropes of the miniature ship between his fingers and contemplated his bookshelves, thinking about how he had felt at the office today, how the donation had changed him. He wondered if his wife could notice the change in his demeanor, the lightness of his footsteps, that new gleam in his eye. Shaking off the urge to check a mirror, to see the change manifested in his flesh, he reached for the encyclopedia collection, selected a particular volume, and settled himself into his reading chair, an overstuffed red leather monstrosity that had been left behind in the house by the last owner. He wasn't sure why he had wanted to keep it; perhaps because his wife had hated it on sight, it reminded her of her father. Lighting a cigarette, he began to read, and began to plan.

*

That weekend, instead of working on his model ship, he pored over medical journals, doing research on his newfound power.

On this particular morning instead of waiting for the bus, he had walked most of the way into the city, his head buzzing with ideas. For the first time since he began his accounting career, he was eager for the day to end. At precisely 3:45pm he swept out of the office and into the streets, his brown shoes and brown suit blending into the business crowd, but instead of going with the press of people heading for the train or various city bus stops, he cut through. He was on a mission. Pushing through the door of the clinic, he ignored the shocked look on the receptionist's face. Steeling his eyes, and smoothing his hair, he sternly demanded to speak to a doctor or the manager, or the director, someone in charge. He projected strength and power, he felt powerful, he felt strong, this was his calling—he could feel it in his bones. The manager of the clinic was exactly who he was hoping to speak to. Shorter by a few inches, with tortoiseshell glasses and a cigarette between his fingers, the clinic manager was very impressed by his strength, by his comprehensive questions, his special requests, and would be in touch. There was so much more that could be donated. So much more help that could be given. Leaving the clinic, he caught a glimpse of his reflection in the plate glass window; his suit jacket hugged his upper body in all the right places, showing off his broad shoulders. His shirt was crisp, the pale blue tie immaculately knotted and complementing the stylish brown of his suit. This wasn't his wife's doing, she wasn't permitted to touch his wardrobe. He had never been obsessed with his looks, but had always been fastidious about his appearance and stood out from the other accountants because of it. He could stand to lose a few inches around the waist; eight years of Tuesday meatloaf dinners were starting to add up. He had only one more stop—a doctor's office down the road recommended by the clinic manager. A discreet one that didn't ask questions, a receptionist that didn't ask for ID, and a doctor that accepted a few bills and then performed a thorough physical. The report would be sent to the clinic manager under strictest confidence. He caught the doctor's assistant sneaking a peek at his body as he dressed and the doctor explained what would come next and smiled to himself, but nothing could compare to the pleasure that was to come.

He was late arriving home, and his wife was drunk and angry, gesturing at him with her martini glass, a gift from their wedding. He hated martinis and she was a cheap drunk. He brushed past her roughly and swept into his study, closing the door on her shouts. If she'd been sober she wouldn't even have noticed his lateness. She was only like this after seeing her friends, she must have had a book club meeting earlier, he'd have to put a stop to that. Her interruptions annoyed him, distracted him from his purpose.

*

Months passed, his life settled back into its familiar routine:

numbers, Tuesday meatloaf, a conference in Milwaukee, greys, browns, beige. Shades. Orderly and utterly predictable. Just like it should be—except for that article in his desk drawer, he read it so many times that his fingers had begun to wear away some of the details. He hadn't forgotten that feeling, deep inside. That private thrill. He made regular visits to the blood bank, donating small pieces of himself every week. But it wasn't enough, the thrill wasn't as strong. He wanted more, he needed more, but his contact was silent. He examined his face in the mirror, he had donated blood earlier that week, and the changes he felt inside were indeed manifesting themselves in his outward self—but it wasn't enough.

Until one day, a voice came over the loudspeaker—a call for him. His heart began to pound. Walking to the common phone, he lifted the goldenrod yellow receiver to his ear and pressed the flashing red line button. He nodded into the phone; of course he would come directly. Confirming the address, he cradled the phone, and walked briskly to his desk. *Tomorrow.* His brow glistened with sweat, but he wasn't afraid, he was exhilarated. He was ready. He jittered his way through the remaining hours of the day like a man who had drunk too much coffee. He didn't remember the bus ride home. As he'd done every day for the last few months, he walked in the front door and locked himself away in his study, saying nothing to his wife. He didn't care if she noticed or not.

*

He stripped himself naked and stood in front of the full-length mirror he had installed a few months ago. He needed to be able to see the change happening within him. The lives he was saving had an impact, he knew it. His eyes were clearer, his hair darker and thicker, his legs stronger, and his body leaner. It was happening. Slowly but surely, he was becoming a better person, more complete despite all of the loss he had put himself through these past few months, but he felt cleaner, newer, refreshed. Polished.

The perfect specimen. The perfect donor.

There was a banging on the door. His wife had finally had

enough, and so had he. She wouldn't get in the way of his purpose. Not when he was so close. Naked, he strode to the door, yanked it open and dragged her inside the room by her always neatly set hair.

*

The next morning, barely hiding his excitement, he dressed comfortably in slacks, loafers and a cotton shirt and then did something he had never done before; he called the office and asked to take the day off. He hadn't taken a vacation in eight years; he was only *not* in the office when it was closed. His request was granted without hesitation. He strode to the foyer, passing the guest bathroom where his wife's corpse lay in ice in the robin's egg blue bathtub. He had smothered her to stifle her gin-soaked accusations, leaving the rest of her body unsullied, and soon she would be a part of his glorious burden, his calling. He would inform the doctor that there was more to be given, she would finally be useful. His appointment was in an hour, soon he would be saving another life, and he could feel whole again. His heart began to pound and he felt a familiar heat start to spread through his groin and stomach. Maybe this time the rush would last longer, the glow would stay with him.

He had so much to give.

ABOUT K.A. MORRIS

Living and working in Vancouver, Canada, K.A. Morris is an author, cat lover, wine drinker and an obsessive horror movie watcher. K.A Morris has published several short stories in various anthologies, and is currently working on a second novel in a series of historical horror tales.

BREATHTAKING VIEWS
BY RACHEL HANSEN

He paused. His hands were clammy. The pen was impossible to grip.

Looking up at the travel agent, who had a huge smile, he reached for a tissue. He thoroughly wiped the pen and his hands until the tissue was falling to pieces. He grabbed the pen once more and hunched in his chair. The pen fell heavy to the paper.

X _Carl Harrisburg_.

He carefully signed at the bottom of the document.

"Great! Great!" The travel agent, Stan—as his flimsy nametag read, snatched the documents off the table, walked them to a large steel cabinet, and locked it behind him. "Alright Chris, are you ready for your vacation?"

Carl shook his head, "I'm Carl."

The agent scooped him up out of the chair and led him to the front door, "Of course, Carl. Wait right here for transport." Carl was deposited on the sidewalk outside the building.

He was left waiting there for almost three hours, stuck outside because the office had closed. He couldn't even call anyone. Carl did not want to miss his ride to the best, and well, _only_ vacation of his entire life. He sat on the curb thinking about how he'd been working since twelve, never making more than the _very_ minimum wage of $4.25. His monthly earnings were only enough to rent a 10x10 apartment in the D Block of the city. It had enough space for a small bed and a coat rack, where he hung all of his clothes. To him, it surely wasn't as bad as the F Block or even G, which was basically a slaughterhouse. Really though, none of this mattered now and it wouldn't matter again until he came back from vacation.

Carl thought it best to start thinking instead of the luxury suite he was about to room in for his trip, about the food and the view of the stars. Mostly, the people living in Blocks A & B were able to afford this package, but the travel company had come up with a special offer for those who could spare a few parts. It was Carl's lucky day.

By signing the contract, he had agreed to give up his right lung in exchange for the trip. Why did he need the two? Cheap breathers, a kind of exterior, artificial lung, were readily available and they were so powerful, they could nearly do the work of both lungs. He already had a few waiting for him back in his 10x10.

He took out the brochure from his pocket and looked at it again, grinning.

"Breathtaking Views!" it read across the top.

The brakes of a car screeched in front of him. He broke his gaze from the brochure and saw a stretch limousine, its front passenger window rolled down. He got up off the curb and peered inside.

"Hop in…" The driver looked down at a cell phone in his lap. "Carl."

Without hesitation, Carl jumped into the back and was met with a bottle of champagne. It was open and half gone, but he didn't care, as he'd never had it before. He took the glass and enjoyed the beginning of his much-deserved vacation.

He wasn't sure of the exact location of the space station, but he had heard that it was close to Mars. With brand new shuttles, developed by a rapidly growing space program in A Block, it only took fifteen hours to get there. The space station was the first of its kind, built to be a second Earth, but the developers had to abandon the project when they realized they couldn't build a space station large enough to hold the world's population. Years later, another private corporation picked up the project and turned it into the ultimate paradise. Within its walls the air was unpolluted and the organic gardens were full of fruits and vegetables now considered rare on planet Earth.

After a short drive, they arrived at the privately owned launching facility. Carl made himself comfortable in his seat on the shuttle. Although he had never been on one, he felt that it was crowded, overstuffed with people who looked to be only from D Block. He didn't recognize them individually, but he could tell by the way they acted and dressed. Carl didn't care though; the seats were more comfortable than any seat in which he'd ever sat. He relaxed and fell asleep.

Carl slept for all fifteen hours of the flight and awoke just as everyone was standing up to disembark. The transport workers handed each vacationer maps, free gifts, and their room keys. Carl stepped off the shuttle onto the flight deck and, along with all the other passengers, admired the beautiful view through the floor-to-ceiling windows. The deck overlooked a vast meadow complete with flowers, real trees, and a winding river. He had never seen any of these things in D Block. Only cement and plastic.

"Right this way, guests!" A young woman spoke sternly, but her face was adorned with a wonderful smile. "My name is Analynn. I will be your hostess for your stay! Please follow me to your rooms." She guided each guest to his or her room and Carl, who was close to last, almost had a heart attack when he entered his. It had to be at least 20x20, maybe even 30x30. He felt total elation. The bed was fresh and *big*! He actually had a sink and a real shower, which he immediately enjoyed. In D Block, he used disposable "bath in a bag" that they were given every other week.

This is the life! he thought. *I'll never forget this.*

After relaxing in his room for a while, he decided he would stroll around the garden he saw earlier. Upon meeting his door, he found it locked from the outside. Carl tried for hours to open it, but was unable to make it budge. He crumbled to the floor and slumped against the wall. Aching to get out, but exhausted, all he could do was stare at the door until he fell asleep.

CLICK

Carl awoke feeling unrested. He noticed a piece of paper had been slid under the door during the night. He picked it up.

8:00 am Breakfast	**1:30 pm** Mud bath
8:30 am Waterfall	**2:30 pm** Endangered Safari
9:00 am Garden	**4:00 pm** Safari clean up
9:30 am Physical	**4:30 pm** Water break
11:00 am NDA paperwork	**5:00 pm** Dinner
12:00 pm Lunch	**5:30 pm** Video testimonial
1:00 pm Desert Oasis w/hot spring	**6:00 pm** Beach paradise

You will be confined to the beach to conclude your first day on vacation! After 6:00 pm, the day is yours! Sit back, relax, and enjoy the real beach that simulates the Caribbean Islands as they were before they were lost over 200 years ago!

Carl made sure to go over the card twice so that he knew what he had to look forward to. Again, he tried the handle and this time, to his relief, the door opened. He followed the signs and made his way to the restaurant for breakfast, but when he arrived, the place was empty. He found some wait staff and they informed him that it was already 9:15.

"You should keep to the schedule!" a busboy lectured. "Otherwise you'll miss out!"

Carl raced to the garden.

It was 9:20 when he arrived. Now he only had ten minutes left in the garden. He found a quiet spot and breathed in the fragrant flowers and freshly cut grass. 9:30 came sooner than he expected and by then, Carl was very hungry.

Analynn guided the guests into the infirmary where the pre-surgery physicals took place. The waiting room was as crowded as the shuttle had been. He was shocked by how many others had made the same deal.

Finally, after signing twenty pages of non-disclosure paperwork, Carl made it back to the restaurant. He thought he could finally have a decent meal, only the wait staff ignored him for ten minutes and his food arrived twenty minutes after that. He tried to savor his meal, but half way into it the group was rushed out to make it to the desert oasis on time. The day went on just like this, with no real time for anything.

The space station offered a sort of "do over" for some species, making the Endangered Safari quite extraordinary. Carl and the other guests were able to see panda bears, Asian Elephants, and other animals that were extinct on Earth. He thought the Safari clean up listed on the schedule had been a mistake, but when they were handed giant shovels and hoses to clear excrement from the enclosures, Carl had to suck it up and clean. He didn't clean quietly.

"I never heard of anyone cleaning on their vacation! Maids clean... not guests!" He flung a pile of elephant shit into the bed of a truck.

"It was in the contract," Analynn replied. She pulled a copy out and pointed to the paper.

"Hmm, I didn't see that," Carl said with disappointment.

"Yeah, it's in the fine print!" She tucked the contract away before he could read any more of what he'd missed.

Dinner, though, was perfect. He was served as if he was the only one in the whole place and got to enjoy his food! Carl even had time for dessert. He ordered a classic apple pie a-la-mode because apples didn't grow on Earth anymore.

In the video testimonial, Carl was asked to recall all the wonderful things he had encountered during his trip. He thought it strange that this was done on the first day when he had hardly experienced much, but he did his best to sound enthusiastic.

"This is worth so much more than a lung! I feel like I got the better end of the deal!"

"That was really nice, Carl," Analynn said while patting his back. "I'm sure they'll use your testimonial in the next promotional video!"

"Wow, that would be great!" Maybe, he thought, he could make some money off of it and get out of D Block.

Again, he signed several pages of paperwork and was then

escorted to the beach. There, he had his own private cabana and the water had a tide, just like the real ocean. The sun shined high in the sky. Carl lay back on a chaise lounge to take it all in.

A drink appeared at his side. It was bright blue, almost glowing, and a giant slice of pineapple hung from the rim. Whatever it was, he found it delicious and before he could finish one they had already delivered another. Six glasses later, Carl again reached for his drink and realized that his brain was telling his arm to move, but it would not. He tried to call for the waiter, but all he could muster was a muffled squeal.

Despite not being able to move, Carl decided he would still enjoy the view. He was paying for it after all. Soon thereafter, a gurney rolled up next to him. He could see the edge of it, but could not move his neck to reveal how it got there or who had brought it. Again, he tried to call out for someone, but nothing resonated in his voice box. Three large men came from behind him, placed him upon the gurney, and strapped him down. Perhaps they knew of his current condition and were going to help? They rolled him off the beach and onto an elevator. The men said nothing as the elevator rose and rose. Carl had no idea where they were going. Finally, the doors opened and they rolled him out into a white, brightly lit room. The men left.

Unable to move, Carl simply waited there, eyes wide open, body completely numb. He heard a rolling clamor mixed with footfalls. The noises came closer and closer. A surgeon, wearing scrubs and a large grin upon his face, appeared above him.

"Carl? Hi, Carl, I am your surgeon today. Can you hear me? Try to say something."

Carl let out a tiny squeak.

"Perfect! Perfect! So you're awake! That's great. This is exactly what we need to happen! So here's the deal, Carl." The surgeon's face went from happy to serious very quickly and Carl became nervous. "You are in a controlled state of suspension. Don't worry, you'll be fine! Calm down, Carl; I can see the fear in your eyes, but really, you are going to live. My god, Jeff, come over here you have to see this guy!" Another surgeon approached. He was covered in blood and he looked down at Carl.

"Holy crap, that's the best I have seen in years!"

Both surgeons walked away from Carl and began whispering to each other. Carl could not make out what they were saying, but it made him even more worried.

"Okay I am back Carl. Let's get through this! So first I am going to crack your chest open and get you fitted for the tubing and the station harness. Hey buddy!" The surgeon chuckled. "You gotta stop making that face. It's going to be fine! You won't feel a thing!"

Carl screamed throughout the whole process, though no one could hear him. The surgeon was wrong. Carl did feel something. He felt his freedom slipping away. When the surgery was over, the surgeon gave him two big thumbs up and the same fucking smile he came in wearing. If Carl could throw up, he would have. The three large men returned and wheeled him out of the operating room.

Then, another long journey. Each room they entered was darker than the last. Finally, they came to a pitch-black hall with a large window to his left. The rolling stopped. The men tried to hook Carl up to something in the dark, but he could hear them cursing about an issue with his chest piece. They took out flashlights and as they successfully connected him, the lights shown upon thousands of dangling bodies. As the men gathered their things, one of them caught a glimpse of Carl's terror-filled eyes. The man leaned in.

"Look, it's nothing against you. It's just that organic filters work best for this environment and well… it takes a lot to keep this place clean. Think of it like this, you're on permanent vacation, you don't ever have to work again."

He smiled at Carl and then shook his head as he walked away. When the door shut behind them, Carl finally stopped trying to scream.

He gave in to the darkness and listened to the room. He could hear the loud hissing of the breathers cycling air through the thousands of lungs. Out the window, he could see Earth. Its fluffy white clouds and bright blue waters looked trouble-free from this high up.

The view was spectacular.

Or, as the brochure had promised, *breathtaking*.

ABOUT RACHEL HANSEN

Rachel Hansen works in the health and wellness field and is currently studying human anatomy and its movement. She has always been drawn to strange things like science fiction, fantasy and horror. This, her first published short story, is just a glimpse into her twisted mind.

ROWAN AND RHYS
BY MICHELLE KILMER

Rhys hated his right arm.

It was attached to him, connected by bone and nerve, a birthright, but it wasn't a part of him. It hung heavier than the left, he was sure of that. The wiggly bits on the end of it twitched uncontrollably. There was a mole in the bend that always grew an obnoxious, thick, black hair. He could do without the tweezing, without the muscles spasms. He could do without the fear that it would strangle him in his sleep.

"Maybe, Rhys, you should get help for the real problem," his twin brother Rowan had said one night over another shared dinner while pointing to his head.

They were identical, but they were different. In Rhys' eyes, Rowan was perfect. He had never felt struggle. He was always getting hired, invited, and laid. He would never understand what it felt like to have an alien limb. Rhys might have been perfect instead, if he had only escaped their mother's womb first. *Four minutes.* It had made all the difference.

Rhys rubbed his temples that, coincidentally, ached. "The problem isn't with my brain."

"There's a name for it. I looked it up." Rowan pulled out his cellphone to recall his search history.

"I shouldn't have told you about any of it." Rhys was no longer hungry. He dumped his uneaten spaghetti into the trash. "Don't look it up anymore."

But Rowan liked to press and now his own mind wouldn't let it go until it knew the answer. "What's it called again?"

85

"Body Integrity Identity Disorder. It isn't that." Rhys hadn't been officially diagnosed. He was hoping to avoid that.

"Are you sure? 'Cause I saw a picture of you and your stupid dead arm next to the definition online!"

"Ha ha. You're making things up."

Rowan laughed. "Yeah, so are you. Like I said, it's all in your fucking head!"

*

Rhys worked from home as an advice columnist. Working from home was, in his opinion, the only option he had. It wasn't easy being around other people. They could tell something was wrong with him. He saw it in their eyes. They saw it in the way his arm hung at his side. But at home he could tell them off, or cheer them on with a few paragraphs of text and without the judgment turned back on him. If he were to give himself advice, it would be *cut it off, or find someone to do it*. But he couldn't trust himself, not when the foreign arm was still attached to him. He needed to hear the words from someone else.

Every answer was findable. The internet was full of the non-unique thoughts floating about the world. His answer was out there. His speaker of the truth was a mouse click away.

If someone else asked me the question, how would I find the answer? he thought. The computer flashed to life. A browser window was already open and waiting. He searched first for the term he'd avoided accepting as his answer, his *issue*; the string of words that kept him from seeking professional help.

Wikipedia *Body Integrity Identity Disorder*

Body Integrity Identity Disorder is a psychological disorder wherein sufferers feel they would be happier living as an amputee.

Okay, maybe this is me, he thought. But knowing it didn't make his arm, or his head, feel right. He still wanted it gone.

Google *My arm doesn't feel like it belongs to me*

Too many results to sort through; 2,290,000 too many. But Rhys clicked through a few pages until he saw the term he was looking for.

Elective amputation.

There it was. Expensive, but eliminative. He could restore balance to his body, his life.

Google *Is amputation painful?*

Amputation-Coalition.org: During the first 72 hours following an amputation, swelling occurs, tissues are stretched, severed nerves are not sending normal impulses to the spinal cord, and many other new realities are being experienced. Tension, fear, anger and denial may be producing a strong emotional "stew" for the new amputee. Physically, this is the time that patients will experience the most severe pain.

Rhys scoffed. "I've already suffered for thirty years." On the same website he found a .pdf detailing others' experiences in life as amputees. He read every word.

Compared to the general population in the U.S., amputees were more likely to report needing the help of another person in one or more activities of daily living.

Rhys wouldn't need help, not even from Rowan.

Google *Amputation surgeon*

Dr. Gordie G. Gordon is a world-renowned surgeon specializing in amputation. He has performed thousands of successful surgeries and helped countless people recover from traumatic limb loss, amputations due to health issues, and less common voluntary amputation.

"Gordie G. Gordon." It sounded even funnier when Rhys said it aloud. "I wonder what the 'G' stands for?"

Regardless of how ridiculous his name sounded, Dr. Gordon practiced in town, not far from Rhys' and Rowan's apartment, and he took Rhys' insurance.

It was meant to be.

*

"Rhys Haversly?" a nurse asked into the waiting room, even though Rhys was the only one there. "Dr. Gordon will see you now."

Dr. Gordon's office was formal enough to instill confidence in Rhys. A medical degree from an unfamiliar college hung in a large frame on the wall behind an oak desk. Filing cabinets had security keypads to access them. The doctor's pen looked heavy and expensive.

The man himself was tall and lean, with wild hair that reminded Rhys of the crazy scientist in *Back to the Future*.

"Sit down," Dr. Gordon said, gesturing to one of two chairs opposite him. "Tell me about yourself."

"Dr. Gord-" Rhys began, but he was stopped by a raised hand.

"My friends call me Gord or 'The Gourd' after a few beers." He winked and then chuckled for longer than was really necessary. "The Gourd" was so thin he barely looked able to fit an apple in his body. He was a man in complete contradiction to his nickname.

"Okay. *Gord*, I'm thinking about getting rid of my right arm."

The doctor smiled. "This is the part where I ask you if you are sure. So, are you? Have you seen a psychologist?"

"I haven't talked to anyone, but I won't be dissuaded. It has never been a part of me. I need the arm to go." Rhys had practiced these lines in front of a mirror. He hadn't needed to practice the conviction, only the strength to say the words. The steady, determined gaze.

The doctor picked up the expensive pen and scribbled illegible notes in a notebook.

"May I ask what you'll do if I say no?"

Rhys shifted in the chair. "Mexico. It'll be more affordable anyway."

"And end up with gangrene? You could lose more than a limb. You'd be better off taking a chainsaw to yourself."

"Obviously there is risk."

"Do you dream of other limbs or body parts being removed?"

"I'm not obsessed with amputation, if that's what you are implying. Just the right arm, nothing else." Rhys felt his face flush red with anger.

Dr. Gordon noticed this. "Calm down, Rhys. I have to ask these questions and you passed the test. Do you want some water?"

"No, thanks. Can we schedule a date then?"

"Hold on. Those were the questions, now here is the spiel. Depression, back pain, non-amputated limb pain, these are all possibilities. Residual limb pain—pain in the remaining section of limb—is almost guaranteed. Seventy percent of amputees surveyed have reported it. Phantom limb pain—pain that occurs where the removed limb used to be as though it is still a part of the body—is also very probable."

"It'll hurt. I know that." *The date, please?*

"Your nerves and your brain have memory and memories engrained since birth are hard to forget." The doctor stood up and walked to a large cabinet.

"I think I'll be all right," Rhys said. He took out his cellphone and opened the calendar.

"It will cost a pretty penny, at least an arm, if not a leg." Dr. Gordon laughed heartily. "A trip to the surgeon wouldn't be complete without a bit of amputation humor, would it?"

He opened the door and removed a tan-colored, plastic arm. With it, he waved at Rhys. "Have you reconsidered a prosthetic?"

Rhys was again becoming angry. He wanted a date for surgery and then he wanted to go back home. "No! My body wants one arm, not two!"

Dr. Gordon shrugged and tossed the arm back into the cabinet. "You may face...a certain amount of discrimination. People may think you incapable of even the most basic of tasks."

That was already true. His dead arm made sure of that. "A date, doctor?"

*

This was how the conversation started. It ended with a serious discussion of cost and a quick glance through a grotesque picture book of amputated limbs and healing surgery scars. And finally, a date was set.

*

That night, Rhys broke the news to his twin.

"I saw a doctor."

"For you head?"

"No!" Rhys threw a pillow with his good arm. "A surgeon."

The look on Rowan's face read as a mix of shock and sadness. "You're really going to do this?"

"I have to. It's going to happen next week."

"Are you sick of being twins? Because I can do something different with my hair."

"This has *nothing* to do with you, Rowan."

"I hardly think so! You're jealous of my good looks, my charm." He pulled a six-pack from the fridge and chugged a beer. It temporarily calmed him.

"You aren't charming and we're identical twins, we look *exactly* the same."

A second beer was already gone.

"Not for fucking long."

*

Rowan drank all night long; something he did when the world wasn't spinning his way. Rhys went to bed, but was awakened by the sound of scissors in the darkness of his room.

He turned on the lamp next to the bed and saw that the closet door was open. Rowan sat on the closet floor, a pile of long-sleeved shirts in his lap. Each one was missing its right sleeve.

"What the hell?" Rhys took the scissors from him and slapped his face.

"You won't be needing these anymore!" Rowan picked up the severed right sleeves and threw them in the air. They fell all around him. One fell on Rhys' head.

"Get the fuck out of my room!" Rhys yelled.

Rowan, drunk and determined to do him one better, decided to get out of his life. He grabbed the keys to his motorcycle, pulled on some jeans, and stumbled toward his bike.

"You can't drive drunk. Rowan, get off the bike!"

He peeled out, nearly crashing before leaving the apartment complex.

Rhys got in his car and followed after him. He'd done this before, too many times.

The accident happened fast. The road was slick from an evening rain and on a corner, the bike slid out from under Rowan. Rhys watched in horror.

"No!" he screamed. If his brother died, half the rent wouldn't get paid. If full rent fell to Rhys, he wouldn't be able to afford the amputation. If he couldn't get rid of his arm, he'd end up killing himself and joining Rowan in the afterlife.

Rowan had to live.

Rhys parked his car and felt for a pulse. He was relieved to find one slowly tromping around in his brother's neck. Looking down at his broken brother, Rhys did the only thing of which he could think.

"Dr. Gordon, hi. It's me, Rhys. Remember how I told you I didn't want my arm to go to waste? I found the answer to that problem, but you have to come quick."

Rowan's right forearm had been badly mangled in the crash. Angles that Rhys had never before seen were created by splintered bones and broken flesh. He took off his flannel nightshirt and tied it as tightly as he could above the largest wound to slow the bleeding.

Dr. Gordon coughed into the phone. "What time is it?"

"Late."

"Are you sure he is a suitable recipient?"

More fucking questions! Rhys' mind screamed. "He's a perfect match! I already know!"

"And you're sure this can't wait until morning?"

"This has to happen right now or we'll miss the opportunity! Get here, please!"

The phone call disconnected. Six minutes flew by. Rowan's pulse grew weaker.

Eight minutes on, a shiny, black Porsche approached and

parked down the road. The headlights illuminated the grim scene. A tall, thin man stepped out of the vehicle and inspected the paint on the driver's side door.

"Dr. Gordon." Rhys was relieved. If it were anyone else, his plan would fail.

"The gravel out here is killer." Dr. Gordon turned from his car to look at the mess that was Rowan. "In more ways than one, I see."

"He's still alive and I'd like for him to stay that way. He pays half the rent and utilities."

"So thoughtful." The surgeon moved closer to the dying man's face. "A twin?"

Rhys nodded.

"Why didn't you tell me about him before?"

"He wasn't useful until this moment."

He felt for a pulse. "Well, he's becoming less useful by the second. To the office, and not in my car!"

*

In the backseat of his own car, Rhys held his brother's head in his lap. He laid his bothersome arm on top of Rowan's damaged one. It looked normal there.

Dr. Gordon drove quickly, but calmly.

At the small clinic, three others waited outside in the cold.

The doctor ran to the door and unlocked it. The others entered and exited a moment later with a gurney, which they rolled to the car. Rhys helped to place his brother on the cart and then followed them inside the still dark building.

"I'll have my team stabilize him so I can get working on you. Be right back, I've got to turn on the lights."

Rhys nodded.

*

Dr. Gordon had taken the stitches out earlier that week. He again urged Rhys to get fitted for a prosthetic for more "seamless societal reintegration". Rhys ate his cereal with his left hand. He paused, set his spoon down, and turned to the next page of the newspaper where his former advice column was printed. Since the removal of his arm, confidence filled him and he'd applied for a job as an office administrator. During the interview, he'd impressed the hiring manager with his one-handed, seventy word-per-minute typing speed. The manager did call him disabled more than once, which hurt Rhys, but he shrugged it off when he was offered the job on the spot.

Rowan flexed the fingers of his new right arm over and over again. He strummed the fingers on the kitchen table. He pushed buttons, flipped switches, opened doors, and picked things up, all as though he was expecting it to fail.

"It's a good arm. I don't know why you hated it so much."

Rhys shrugged an even-feeling shrug. "Suits you better."

Rowan sat on the couch and steadied a set of tweezers in his left hand over the mole on his new arm. "This fucking hair won't stop growing though. It's like every time I blink, it's back."

"I know," Rhys said with a smile as he caressed the stump of his right arm. "I know."

Rowan pulled the hair out with a quick upward motion.

Rhys felt a twinge where his arm used to be.

*

That night he was pulled from sleep by a tightening around his neck. He reached for his bedside lamp and when it illuminated the room, there Rowan was, in bed with him. Rowan was in a deep sleep, but his new right arm was very much awake. It gripped Rhys' neck with intent to kill.

"Rowan!" Rhys screamed. He struggled to pry his old fingers open with his one hand. "You're killing me!"

ABOUT MICHELLE KILMER

Michelle Kilmer is a horror enthusiast from Seattle, WA. When she is not writing, she enjoys hiking and camping, playing guitar, lifting weights, dressing up in "full gore" to attend zombie-related events, web design and gaming. Her writing portfolio includes the novel *When the Dead*, the novel *The Spread: A Zombie Short Story Collection*, and a writing collection entitled *Last Night While You Were Sleeping*. Several of her short stories can be found in other books including *Roms, Bombs, and Zoms* from Evil Girlfriend Media and *A Very Zombie Christmas* from ATZ Publications.

After many adventures, she currently lives in Southern California with her boyfriend, a friendly neighbor dog, and a fear of the dark.

WITH ALL MY...
BY PANDEM BUCKNER

"You know you're a hero, right?" Maggie said, holding my hand.

"I know," I said, "but you'd think heroes would get better food." I grimaced at the tray of hospital "food" in my lap. "I don't think that meatloaf was made this decade."

"You only have a couple days of hospital food, then you can go home." Maggie ruffled my hair. I looked up at her with puppy-dog eyes; she never could resist that. "Fine, Mark," she sighed. She grinned, despite her faux exasperation. "I'll bring you some pizza later."

When she grinned, I saw the gap in her teeth. It had always been there, at least for the eight years I'd known her. I'd always thought it was cute before, but today . . . I don't know. It just wasn't cute anymore.

I pushed the stand away from the bed. "At least the bed is comfy." I lowered it a little, so I wasn't quite sitting up anymore. "Any word on Eric?"

"Doin' good, hero-bro!" Eric said from the door, walking into the hospital room. I was surprised; I hadn't thought he'd be out of bed so soon after the surgery.

"Are you supposed to be up already?"

"Nope! But I had to come see you!" He stepped closer to the bed. Maggie let go of my hand and moved to a chair by the window. Eric picked up the hand she abandoned and held it in his, which were cold and a little pale. "Seriously, man, you saved my fuckin' life."

I tried to play it off. "Don't get mushy on me, dude, it wasn't a big deal." But it was, and we both knew it. Two years ago, Eric had been in a car accident that broke his arm and some of his ribs. His spleen was damaged too, but nobody noticed it then. Later, when he started getting sick, they found nearly half his spleen had become necrotic and needed to be removed. Problem was, you can't function with just half a spleen, you need at least 75%, so I volunteered to give up a quarter of mine to him. "It's what you do for family."

"Yo, *you* did it though, bro. You didn't see Lucy flouncin' her ghetto ass in here to give up her spleen, did you?" There was definitely no love lost between my brother and sister. "She'll break off a piece of ass for anybody looks at her right, but when her brother needs-"

"Let it go, Eric," I said, seeing Maggie's raised eyebrow. She liked Lucy, and we didn't begrudge Lucy for being sexually liberated. It bothered Eric, for some reason I didn't know. I'd never cared enough to learn why. "Don't make me regret saving your ass."

"Alright, for now." Eric winced and held his side. "I better get back to my bed."

Eric was one of those guys that always downplayed his own pain. For him to wince visibly, I knew he was really hurting. "Maggie, help him back?"

"I'm good," Eric said, and tried to wave her away. The motion of waving made him wince again; this time she saw it.

"You're getting help, Eric, accept it," she said, and pulled him into leaning on her shoulder. I watched them shuffle towards the door, mostly because my wife had such a cute ass. Not too big, not too small . . . well, I thought, maybe a little big. Could be better, but still pretty good.

At the door, Eric let go of Maggie. "Thanks, Mags," he said, and looked at her for a long time.

"What?" she and I both said.

Eric shook his head. "Nothin'. Drugs must be kickin' in. For just a second, you looked — different."

Maggie touched her hair. She'd been with me all night before the surgery and all day leading up to it; I don't think she left the hospital at all. "It's probably my hair," she chuckled. "It's usually not so rough."

"Yeah, that must be it," Eric replied. His smile was weak; I couldn't tell if that was from the pain or the medication. "You need anything, I'm down the hall."

"Me too," I said as he turned away. As soon as he was gone, I asked Maggie, "Does he seem okay to you?

"He's probably scared still," she replied, sitting down on my bed. "He almost died. *Would* have died, without you. That's gotta rattle him a bit."

"Yeah, I guess," I replied, and sank back against the pillows. Maggie snuggled up against me, carefully avoiding the incision. I put my arm around her and buried my face in her coarse hair. "That's gotta be it."

*

The banner was a bit much, I thought.

"Welcome home, Mark!" the small crowd by the banner shouted. Maggie was at my side, letting me lean on her as I walked into our house. Before I left the hospital, the doctors told me I was strong enough to go home and walk alone, but I felt . . . . off, somehow. Lessened. Like something important was gone. With nothing medically wrong, though, they couldn't keep me any longer.

"Thanks, guys," I said. I wobbled over for a group hug. "You didn't have to do this for me, though. It really wasn't a big deal."

"All we did was show up to eat cake!" Andrew, a fellow security guard, said. "Ain't like it's your birthday!"

"You did good, man," Paul said, clapping my shoulder. He was the supervisor at my security site, and the guy who'd gotten me the job in the first place. "I don't know if I coulda done it."

"It was just a piece of my spleen," I replied. I looked at my wife, who was talking to another coworker. The way she stood, with a drink in one hand and her wrist against her hip, her hand jutting out from it at an angle, was weird to me. It was how she normally stood at gatherings like this, but somehow it looked fake, posed. Like that's how she *thought* she should stand, rather than how she naturally stood. "I'll never even miss it."

"I dunno," Paul said, "I think I'd feel like somethin' was missin'."

When Eric got there, he was unusually quiet. Everybody noticed it; everybody commented on it. Maggie and I both chalked it up to his near-death experience, and everybody seemed to understand and gave him space. He was still a little pale, and sat at the end of the sofa alone. Every time I glanced his way, he was looking at either me or Maggie. Sometimes he'd talk with one of our friends, but never for long. All I could do was hope he snapped out of it soon.

*

"Guess what, honey?" Maggie said from the bathroom.

"What?" I was already lying in bed, watching TV. It was my last free night before going back to work.

"You can have strenuous activity again," she said, standing in the doorway in a bathrobe.

I raised my eyebrow at her. "You have something in mind?"

"Oh, honey," she giggled, and dropped the robe. "I got *plenty* in mind."

I watched her walk, naked as the day she was born, to the bed. I'd known Maggie for eight years and been married for six, and Maggie had always been as beautiful to me as the day we met. But that night . . . something was different. Maggie had always been a bit curvy, but now I could tell she'd gained some weight since we first met. Her bosom hung a little lower than before, her nipples not as perky as they'd been. Her hips and waist didn't look as distinct as they used to be; her thighs definitely had the start of some cellulite going. *So she's gotten a little older*, I told myself as she slunk seductively to the bed. *So have you, and she's still the woman you love*. Besides, noticing those flaws didn't stop the visible reaction in my pajama pants.

"I've missed you," she said as she climbed onto the bed, straddling my legs and stopping with her face right above my lap. "And it looks like you missed me too . . ."

"What do you think?" I replied with a smile.

We made love that night. It was true, I had missed her, but . . . somehow, things were different. When I felt her teeth on me where I generally prefer not to feel teeth, I pulled her up for hard kisses instead and let her ride me. She rode me for as long as I could hold out, which wasn't as long as usual–she only came twice, not her usual four or five before I gave in. We both got off, so it was satisfactory, but it just wasn't the same. Before we fell asleep, Maggie asked if I was okay. I blamed it on being nervous about going back to work and not having gotten any in a while. My explanation seemed to placate her; she went to sleep shortly after.

I lay awake for hours, wondering what was wrong with me.

*

Three weeks later, I came home from a doctor's appointment around 7 p.m. Maggie had insisted on me going. In those three weeks, our lovemaking had only worsened in quality, and she said I seemed disinterested and listless around the house. Like I was "just going through the motions," she said. The doctor ran some tests the week before, and gave me the results that day: nothing was wrong, my body was working fine, even down a quarter of a spleen. Dr. Quigley offered to refer me to a therapist if need be.

When I got home, Eric's car was parked in front of the house.

That wasn't too unusual; Eric had been over once or twice a week since the transplant. He usually checked to make sure I was at home first; for him not to have done so was odd. I got worried that maybe something was wrong with Mom, something he had to tell me in person. I gunned it into the driveway, ran to the house, and flung the door open, scared Mom had died.

Maggie was seated on the couch. Eric was besides her, laying down with his head in her lap . . . and he was . . .

Eric was *crying*.

"Oh God, what's happened? Is it Mom?" I asked.

Eric raised his head just enough to shake his head. Maggie eased herself out from under his head and gracefully placed a pillow under him. We left him there, sobbing to himself, as she took my arm and pulled me into the kitchen.

I hated when she did that now. It had seemed kind of assertive and take-charge-y before, but now it felt more like I was being guided, like a dumb kid. In the kitchen, I gently shrugged off her grasp. "What's going on?" I whispered. "I can count on one hand the number of times I've seen Eric cry!"

"He's scared and alone, Mark," she whispered back. "He almost died! It made him realize how lonely he is, how he feels like he hasn't done anything with his life."

"Hasn't done anything? That drunken womanizer does *plenty*, trust me."

"Nothing *real*, Mark, nothing lasting. Nothing that feels like a real achievement to him. Nothing he can point to and be proud of."

"So why didn't he come to me about it?"

"He didn't think you'd understand. Seems like he was right."

I knew she had a point, but she just seemed so *smug* about it.

*

Two months later, I was the one crying.

Maggie and I hadn't had sex in weeks. The last couple of times we'd tried, well, my spirit was willing but my flesh was weak, and really, my spirit hadn't been all that willing. Every day brought some new aspect of Maggie that I had somehow never noticed before, or I used to find cute, or just somehow overlooked. Had she changed, gradually but drastically, and I'd never noticed? I didn't know, and not knowing hurt my head because it didn't hurt my heart like I thought it should have.

I was a mess when Maggie found me, drunk and crying,

almost passed out on the floor of the den, surrounded by pictures of us. There were pictures from the night we met, from our first few dates, from our wedding, from our married life. They were scattered around me, ripped out of albums or printed out and shredded. And there I was in the middle of them all, ripped to the gills, my t-shirt stained with spilled beer, a bottle spilling from under my fingers, sobbing into the carpet.

"Jesus H. Christ, what happened in here?!" Maggie demanded.

How could I explain to her that I had been looking for the woman I loved? The woman I'd loved from the first moment I saw her? The woman I'd married and promised my life to? The woman who'd promised her life to me?

Even worse, how could I explain that, in all my searching, I didn't find that woman?

"Maggie," I slurred. "I lo-"

I couldn't say it. I choked on the words. Choked, and threw up.

"You're fucking pathetic," Maggie sneered, and stormed off.

*

When Maggie told me she was moving out, three months after that, I wasn't surprised at all.

"Where are you gonna go? You don't make enough to live on your own."

"What do you care?" she snapped. She didn't even stop packing long enough to talk.

"I . . . I do care," I stammered. It was a lie. We both knew it.

"Eric said I could stay with him until I get on my feet."

"*Eric?* You're gonna live with my fucking *brother?*" I didn't feel the anger in my words. I should have, but I didn't. I couldn't.

"Eric *needs* me, Mark," she replied, dragging her suitcase down the stairs. "You don't need me. You need therapy and Alcoholics Anonymous. You . . . you don't even *want* me anymore." The door closed behind her with a soft click.

I couldn't argue. She was right.

*

A month later, we were divorced. She didn't want the house, didn't want alimony, didn't want anything from me. We communicated through lawyers.

A year later, Maggie and Eric got married. I didn't go to the wedding. I spent the day like I'd spent the year before it: getting drunk and fucking women I didn't love in the futile hope that I *could* love them, that I might find some spark of even the ability to love somewhere deep within me.

I didn't.

I'd given it to my brother.

ABOUT PANDEM BUCKNER

Pandem Buckner has been writing strange stories and poetry for a very long time, and finally got around to hating the world enough to share them. He loves comic books, video games, collectible card games, and not going outside. He lives in the Seattle area with his daughter. He is the author of currently-available children's book *Princess Catherine and the Toy Thief* (with artist Noelle Marie) and upcoming novella *The Burial*.

WHAT A FATHER WOULD DO
BY CHERYCE CLAYTON

"What if it's a lie? What if I wake up in a hotel room in a bathtub full of ice?" Chianti whispered in a nervous joke. They were sitting in the back of a city bus, her meds were wearing off, and she kept her body twisted away from the interior of the bus and the seven other passengers. She stared at Brian and watched him not watch her.

"Baby, it's not a scam. You're not going to wake up in a bathtub. He's a real doctor with a real office, you'll see," Brian replied, only a little annoyed. "We go in, the nurse talks to us, we sign the papers, we each get a kidney removed, and then we get married and live happily ever after."

Chianti wished he didn't sound so impatient every time he reassured her.

"And you'll be there for me? You won't leave my side?"

"I promise I will be right there in the operating room with you the whole time. Nothing will go wrong," Brian answered again without looking away from the bus window. "Our stop."

The doctor's office was in a nicer neighborhood than Chianti had known existed in the city. Deep, lush lawns with hired help in uniforms weeding flower beds beside old women in hats, garden gloves, and pearls. The walk from the bus stop to the office was three blocks and they passed seven large houses, a coffee shop, two art galleries, and a chiropractor's office before turning north on Salazar Way. The nondescript medical clinic was set back from the road with a black glass entryway and cascading baskets of baby blue forget-me-not flowers and dead petunias on either side of the door.

Chianti read the text on the door.

The Salazar Charitable Clinic
Dr. T. Harris
Dr. A.B. Trevino
A. Fish, NP

"Right this way," a nurse greeted them walking in the door without asking their names and led them into a plush sitting room decorated with a red leather couch and chair, an old desk with no chair, and wall to wall books. She couldn't see the titles in the dim light from a single dirty window and a green, shaded lamp.

"Did you have any questions?" the nurse asked. She wore a starched white uniform, which Chianti found reassuring. Chianti glanced quickly to read her name tag, "Abigail" before pretending to study the books, again.

Chianti shook her head. She was glad when the nurse didn't mention the mandatory counseling session, simply handing them each a clipboard with the spots requiring signatures neatly checked in red.

It was five pages of legal words that she didn't try to read. Chianti waited as Brian worked his way through one page at a time and then moved the paper towards her for each new signature. Her form took him ten minutes to read as she looked out the window at an empty bird feeder. His form took him twice as long to read and at one point he got up and left the room to discuss something with the nurse before returning and signing each page with a sigh.

She knew she should read the papers, knew that donating a kidney to some rich person and trusting to have the promised money deposited into their bank account was not the smartest move she had ever made. But Brian looked out for her, he took care of getting her paperwork straightened out with her medical, he let her stay at his apartment, he helped her to not feel crazy and alone. They were getting married, she had the little chip of diamond in a ring to remind her that he loved her. This was scary and if he was distant or almost rude she told herself it was because he was scared too.

"I'll need your jewelry and personal concerns," the nurse said and offered her a large manila envelope.

"Oh," Chianti whispered. She removed the ring Brian had given her the day before they decided to donate a kidney each to make enough money to move out of the city. The day they had packed up his little apartment and put it in storage until he had the money for back rent. The day after her medical had finally come through.

She put the ring into her small purse and her purse into the envelope. Brian was putting his wallet into a second envelope. He smiled to her and she thought he might make a little joke, but the nurse took the envelopes from him and walked to the door.

"Five minutes enough?" the nurse asked and Chianti wanted to say no, wanted to ask for an hour, but the fear of speaking to a stranger kept her quiet and Brian just nodded.

He held her. He whispered love and promised warm beaches, and after five minutes he thanked her with tears in his eyes before the nurse came in and led her to a small undressing room and had her climb onto on a metal table.

The cold shocked her and she wanted to ask for a blanket as she lay there completely nude and more vulnerable than even her father had made her feel.

"How are you today?" an older man asked from above her head and Chianti flinched and fought the scream in her throat.

"Here," he continued as he moved a face mask toward her face, but her look of fear must have surprised him because he turned to the nurse and in the same quiet voice asked "Has she been counseled?"

"Yes," was the reply, without a glance down to see her, and Chianti watched as the woman worked at setting out small steel tools on a tray she could see in her peripheral vision. "Read her file, severe social anxiety. Kid's a shut in, had to mail her Valium just to get her here."

"Oh," the older man said and turned back toward Chianti, "This will calm you down, like at the dentist, just breathe deeply and everything you're afraid of will go away."

The mask lowered over her face as Chianti gulped the latex-scented gas.

"Count back slowly from...." The room went black, the fear faded away, and Chianti realized she had made a mistake. Memories from the last three months flooded her mind and every doubt she had ever had about Brian filled her with a sense of empty sadness.

*

"Are you going the club this Saturday?" a voice said in the dark.

Chianti heard a metal clink, a wet gurgle, and an electronic beeping.

"Wasn't planning on it, why?" The old man's voice came from above her as Chianti felt a pinching sensation just under her left eye. She wanted to blink, tried to scream, needed them to acknowledge her. But she was frozen, the mask was gone, and she could see a faint light in the room as the pinching sensation drug under her left eye and then above.

"Prime rib at the restaurant," the first voice commented, "it's usually pretty good."

A heavy, wet, red form was removed from Chianti's face and she tried to focus her eyes to the sudden light overhead. She could see one blurry man setting aside something carefully.

"Eyes?" the older man asked and Chianti thought they had noticed her attempts to blink away the blur.

"Astigmatism is too bad," the doctor above her said. "Increasing her sedation."

And the pinching tug started just below her throat, moving down between her breasts. Chianti wished they would put the mask back on her. She didn't want to see the doctor. She fought to not think about the blurred form she had seen lifted off her face. She wanted to scream and not admit to herself why she couldn't blink.

"I don't like their prime rib, they over cook it," the doctor finally replied. "Prep the boyfriend. I'm going to take the liver and lungs together and then this one can be chilled. Hand me the saw."

Hail, Holy Queen, Mother of Mercy, our life, our sweetness and our hope! Chianti tried to block out the sound of the saw with a prayer from childhood.

To you we cry, poor banished children of Eve; to you we send up our sighs, mourning and weeping in this valley of tears. The pain turned to light and bloomed pure white before everything started to fade.

Most gracious, mercy, baby Jesus. O sweet Virgin Mary! And the empty sadness returned.

*

He was almost out of time when he found Chianti at the bus stop. His daughter was dying. Cystic Fibrosis was eating her lungs. Her tissue type was rare but more devastatingly, the hepatitis he had given her mother during pregnancy had damaged her liver and prevented her from being allowed on the donor list for new lungs and a liver.

He had learned to read the color coding of the state insurance medi-badge bracelets, or at least how to scan for his daughter's blue-blue-white-blue-red in the upper left corner. It pissed him off that healthy people didn't wear their medi-badges; only the disabled who wanted free bus rides, and the crazies, wore them openly for anyone to read.

Chianti was a match for his daughter. Chianti would save her life. And luckily Chianti had been such a fucking mouse that it was almost too easy to convince her to donate a single kidney. He had lied. He had said he was doing the same. Everything was a lie. Brian never felt guilty. His daughter Annie was his only reason for living. She was the only good thing he had ever done and he was going to save her life.

"Your girlfriend was a bit spooked," the anesthesiologist said by way of greeting.

"Yeah, she's afraid of her own shadow," Brian replied from

the cold metal gurney.

"You didn't tell her," the doctor said in mild rebuke.

"She volunteered to donate a kidney," Brian said, waiting for the gas.

"Then it's not really assisted suicide with organ donation, now is it?" the doctor continued to rebuke, standing above Brian's naked form.

"Her liver and lungs go to my daughter, that's our deal," Brian insisted and felt his penis react to his stress. He hoped the prick of a doctor was enjoying the show.

"Just as soon as we harvest your heart, liver, and kidneys to pay for the procedure," the doctor replied, lowering the mask.

*

"Do you mind if I take a slice fresh?" Doctor Trevino asked from inside the cooler.

"Of course, why don't you start with the boy's left iliopsoas and cut enough to share," Dr. Harris replied as he finished taping up the seventh red icebox for immediate transport to the hospital. The transport crew waited for the harvested organs in the clinic lobby as Abigail finished the paperwork.

"Think the little girl will receive the transplant well?" Trevino asked when his colleagues returned from the lobby. He offered a plate of not quite chilled *Brian* to share.

"I hope so, it's so romantic, their sacrifice," Abigail said.

"The girl didn't know," Trevino commented as he delicately picked up a carpaccio slice and dabbed it in balsamic vinegar.

"There is that," Harris replied with a mock toast of his own bit of meat.

ABOUT CHERYCE CLAYTON

Cheryce used to be a ghost but is now independent. She writes,

Space Opera, SF, Horror, Erotica, Fantasy - whatever bubbles out.

She has a webcomic - Tales from the Zombie Apocalypse. www.facebook.com/TalesfromtheZombieApocalypse

Her longer stories and books are on Amazon. www.amazon.com/Cheryce-Clayton/e/B00O07C20K/

Find her on FaceBook; she doesn't bite. www.facebook.com/cheryceclayton

HEART-SHAPED BOX
BY STEPHANIE BISSETTE-ROARK

Talia grimaced and tried not to fidget against the hard plastic stirrups that braced her feet apart. She glanced down the length of her Pepto-Bismol colored gown to where Dr. Warren's balding head bobbed, almost out of sight behind the false privacy of the cloth draped over her knees.

"Well?" she asked, the question surprisingly loud in the small examination room. "Do you feel anything?"

Dr. Warren paused, wrist-deep inside her. "Nothing out of the normal, all things considered."

All things considered...he meant for a young woman who'd had her workings removed. Donated, one could say. Though, Talia's bank account told otherwise. It'd been a transaction, nothing more.

She'd never needed the thing before and financial security fulfilled her more than that troublesome organ ever could. Let someone else deal with it. Maybe they'd have better luck.

Dr. Warren sat back and pulled off his gloves with a hearty snap. "The surgical site appears to be healing well, and as long as you don't lift anything heavy or exert yourself for the next couple of weeks, you should experience a full recovery." He wheeled over towards his tray of shiny, silver instruments. "You can sit up now," he stated.

Talia complied, lifting her feet out of the stirrups. She levered herself up with a frown, hating the way the lubricant puddled beneath her. In the over air-conditioned space, the fluid cooled quickly into a mucousy smear of chilly glop.

"We'll still expect you to come in every so often for pelvic exams," Dr. Warren continued. "And just because you no longer have a uterus does not mean the threat of cancer is one-hundred percent absent. Preventative check-ups are still required to ensure good health."

Talia waved a hand at him. "I know…I know all that. They explained all this months ago, before the operation. But what I want to know is…did they get it all?"

"Excuse me?"

Talia pushed her glasses higher up the bridge of her nose. "I mean, is any of it there? Did the surgeons miss anything, some bit or bob still rattling around inside?"

Dr. Warren frowned. "You're worried about possible surgical complications?"

She shook her head, her rope of braided auburn hair seconding the denial.

"No. I'm worried they didn't get it all."

Dr. Warren arched a furry, salt-and-pepper eyebrow. "Why do you think that?"

How to tell him? How to explain the rising sense of apprehension; the little out of place changes she'd noticed? And the dreams. Did she dare tell him about those?

Talia took a deep breath. "I'm just worried that something went wrong."

"Ms. Preston," he began, switching to the clinical, condescending sympathy cultivated from years of dealing with the public, "you've gone through a very serious surgery. It's completely natural for the body and mind to experience certain after-affects. Hormone levels aside, it will take time for you to adjust." Dr. Warren scooted forward to pat her knee, his icy fingers raising gooseflesh as they curled towards her inner thigh. "If this is a concern about when you can resume your normal sexual practices—"

Talia jerked away and hopped off the opposite side of the examination table. In the corner beneath the inspirational cat poster, she forced a reassuring smile.

"It's nothing," she lied. "Just nerves, I guess."

Dr. Warren eyed her a moment. "If you'd like, I can get you in contact with a professional friend of mine who could speak with you further about your fears."

Talia was shaking her head before he'd even finished his sentence.

"No. Thank you. I appreciate the offer, but it's like you said, I just need some time to get a handle on things."

*

Talia's car squealed into the parking spot in front of the gas station just as the sun slipped below the horizon. In a rush to get out, she nearly choked herself on the seat belt. She hurried inside, flip-flops clip-clapping across the freshly-mopped linoleum floor towards the rear of the shop. Once there, she snatched up what she'd need for the night and dashed to the register.

The night clerk skimmed bored eyes over her stash.

"Damn girl," he drawled, "when are those finals going to be over?"

"Hmm?" she asked as she fished for exact change.

He rung up the boxes of energy drinks and instant coffee piled before him and stuffed them in a crinkly, plastic bag.

"The tests...for your university courses," he clarified. "You should be careful. These all-nighters will do your head in."

Talia handed over the cash. It sat, balled up in the palm of her hand, all wrinkly and covered in sweat.

"Don't worry," she assured him as he relieved her of her money. "I'll be careful."

Even to her ears, the statement rang false.

*

Alone in her tiny apartment, Talia stripped down to her skivvies and jimmied the ancient window open to invite in the chill. It lanced across her skin, leaching warmth in its wake. Shivering, she forced herself to huddle near the gap as she downed her giant mug of equal parts coffee and energy drink, near scalding her throat in the process.

The first few hours passed easily enough. Though, too soon, she ran out of corners to scrub and towels to fold, and all the dishes sat—clean and shiny—in their little Ikea cubby holes. Despite herself, fatigue set in; the edges of her perception grew fuzzy and filled to capacity with irate, squiggly lines.

Talia fought it off for a time, jammed earbuds into her head and cranked the dubstep while she paced back-and-forth across the front room, annoying her neighbors below. She walked as if she could walk across the whole entire earth; outpacing the moon as she raced towards the sun. She walked as if the steps could actually take her somewhere. As if they could lead her home.

He found her, like he always did. Came to her like a phantom—because that was what he was—and lulled her into something close to contentment. She hated him for this; hated him because she knew he would take it away.

Caught on the vestiges of those moments, she both loved and despised him. And he knew it. And he fed.

When she woke, Talia crawled into the bathroom, dragging herself over impossibly-white tiles to heave herself into the shower. This early in the morning, there was plenty of hot water, and so she let it run, sluicing over her corpse-blue skin made almost iridescent beneath the unforgiving glare of fluorescent light. Numbness dissolved as feeling returned, accompanied by a pain so deep, so pure, it throbbed heavy in her core.

She glanced down, expecting to see drops of red tinging the water pink. Nothing was there. Nothing could be seen past the dark curtain of her hair.

So she sat, curled in about herself until her flesh turned scarlet beneath the downpour. Then she sat further still, until the skin he'd skimmed his kisses over undulated into thick wrinkles; a private, impenetrable landscape.

*

Dr. Cameron Triskel turned out to be a woman, though by her

gender-neutral name it could have been either. She sat across from Talia, a middle-aged conglomeration of Midwest fashion sense and east coast pretension. Her pale blue three-piece looked well-pressed, if a bit fuddy-duddy. Overall, she reminded Talia of a middle school teacher, or some out-of-work broadcaster.

"Why don't you start?" the doctor asked, her sanguine grin not entirely eclipsed by the cup of coffee she nursed.

Talia tried not to shrug. Would such a move make her seem defensive? Indecisive? She clutched at the hem of her sweater to still her need to fidget with the bandages it concealed.

"I don't know what to say," she admitted.

"Why don't you start with the first thing that comes to mind?"

Talia let go of her sweater to clutch at the mounded territory of her stomach. "I think I am changing."

With a quick, rasping scrape of her pen, Dr. Triskel devirginized a sheet of crisp, yellow legal paper. "What do you mean by *changing*?"

"This is going to sound crazy…"

"Try me," Dr. Triskel urged.

Talia sighed. "I think I'm pregnant."

That got the psychologist's silver fountain pen to pause. Dr. Triskel frowned, ruining the previously smooth cake of her foundation. "You believe you're pregnant?"

"Yes," Talia admitted with a nod. "I told you I'd sound crazy."

Dr. Triskel stared surprisingly warm, brown eyes across the large, mahogany desk at her. "And why do you think you are with child?"

"I've been seeing a man—"

"Sexual intercourse in your state can hardly find you with child, Ms. Preston."

"Just Talia."

"Alright. Talia. As I was saying, considering your medical condition, it would be scientifically impossible for you to sustain a life. You are aware of this, correct?"

Talia shook her head. "No. You don't understand. When I

say I've been seeing a man, I mean I've *literally* been seeing him…in my dreams. He's not real. But he keeps stalking me or courting me or something and…I mean, just look!" Talia lifted up her sweater to expose the ample dome of her belly. "How the hell do you explain this?!"

Dr. Triskel took another sip of her caramel-flavored coffee. The sickly-sweet scent rioted across Talia's senses, making her nauseous. Then again, everything seemed to make her nauseous nowadays.

"Certain medical and psychological states can mimic the signs of pregnancy."

"You're not listening!" Talia yelled, jumping to her feet to stare down at the other woman. "I am telling you there is something inside me, something real and alive!"

Dr. Triskel's face was as blank as her notepad had been. "Is that the reason you resorted to self-harm?"

Talia clenched her fists at her side, testing the give of the stitches at her wrists.

"I didn't want to die, if that is what you are asking. I just…" Talia let her thoughts trail away. With a defeated sigh, she sat. "I'm not crazy. I'm not," she added, as if saying it twice would make it true.

Dr. Triskel scratched her shiny, silver pen across the paper. The chafing sound scrambled into every corner of the room, filling it up with its harsh, clinical murmurations.

"I'm going to suggest a series of medications," she deigned to inform. "Something to stabilize your mood and help you get some rest."

Fear lanced into Talia's core. "Haven't you been listening?" she implored. "I don't want to sleep. I can't."

Dr. Triskel's smile was anything but sympathetic. "We can do this the easy way or the hard way, Ms. Preston. Which do you prefer?"

Talia turned away. It didn't matter. Nothing mattered anymore.

*

In the dim of day, Talia's usual industrial, taupe-colored room mutated into a strange almost-pink, like dissected tissue. She lay on her plastic-covered mattress and watched the weak rays of light recede across the viscera-like walls, fleeing through the gap of the window's frame to leave her in shadow.

She shifted—or tried to—the bindings about her wrists pulling her up short. As preventatives measures went, they'd been a tardy postscript to her care. In a complete lack of available sharp corners or serrated edges, Talia'd had to gnaw her own stitches to get the blood flowing again.

They'd found her quick enough, drugged her into submission and trussed her to the bed. She lay there now, timing the passage of moments through the weak stopwatch of her heart. That bulb of muscle pulsed—slow and sluggish—resignation and medication lending it a false calm.

He took his time; he knew he had the luxury. Talia watched with sedative-laden eyes as his form separated from the surrounding dark and approached, bearing the chill of evening with him.

She wouldn't fight; she'd promised herself that much. What dignity was there in struggle? It'd never saved her before and had only spurned past attackers into animalistic realms of pleasure.

And maybe that was why he'd chosen her; because she was good at giving up. In the end, she deserved the lust and the hate; had always known she'd been the sinful, dirty thing that stronger souls coveted.

Unlike the other times, Talia was awake when he forced himself inside. His dark form wavered at the foot of her bed, a strobe of after-images haunting her gaze. She turned away; tried not to groan against the steady, pulsating pressure that erupted from her core.

Hot slickness pooled beneath her; the muggy, meaty smell of copper saturating her senses. Talia writhed against the lancing pain; her panted breaths a puff of ghostly condensation. Something tore away. It squirmed inside, distending the confines of her lower stomach.

Talia's muscles seized, seeming to cleave her in two. She screamed, the sound reverberating back to her in the tiny room. The hazy phantom strained at the root of her as fever-hot sweat slid across her forehead, cooling quickly in the icy chamber. Despite herself, she pushed, aiding in the evacuation. As her gaze grew dim, she felt the last of him pull away, and with him a part of herself.

*

The creature curled into the protective hold of its father and turned new, unblinking eyes towards its past. The female lay on her back, the blood-slickened bed steaming in the icy chamber. Her eyes—a mirror to the creatures' own—stared wide and glassy towards the being; any warmth she might have offered dripped a tacky staccato onto the floor.

The two stood in silent witness for some time, paying the only homage their kind knew how. Then—once the tether had grown desiccated and cold—they pulled away, dissipating like phantoms into the shiny, silver night.

ABOUT STEPHANIE BISSETTE-ROARK

Stephanie Bissette-Roark's short fiction has appeared in numerous horror anthologies as well as Every Day Fiction. When not writing, her hobbies include gardening, thrift-store shopping, roleplaying and adding to her ever-increasing stash of tea. She lives in Tacoma, WA with her husband, Matthew, and their two wrasslin' cats.

BITS AND BOBS
BY KAYLEIGH MARIE EDWARDS

Steven Plunkett stared at Doctor Leanne Linstrum's expression from his side of the desk and groaned inside. He had seen that same expression on a dozen faces over the last couple of years, and he knew what was coming. All remaining hope of his dream plummeted to the pit of his stomach. *Don't say it*, he thought, staring at her forehead as he willed her to change her mind. *Just don't say it.*

"I'm sorry Mr. Plunkett, we just feel that this isn't a good fit for you." Doctor Linstrum cocked her head to the side in that oh-so-sympathetic way he had seen so many times. He closed his eyes, feeling the tears rise up his throat. Steven rubbed his palms on his knees, leaving damp imprints, and smiled a tight-lipped smile. *Just leave*, he commanded himself. *Keep your dignity.*

He rose to his feet, steadying himself as his heart pounded in his ears. It knocked so hard against his ribcage that he wobbled a little as he stood. He turned and shuffled towards the door, his shoulders hunched as they always were, and turned back towards her. She smiled with sympathetic eyes and opened her mouth, about to say something.

"Well, fuck you then," he said, and then hunched out of her office, taking care to avoid eye contact as her mouth dropped open. *Damn it! I said, keep your dignity!* Steven scolded himself.

Steven hadn't been in Tennessee for long and already his trip was wasted. As a child, he had obsessed over all things morbid. As a teenager, he'd had his first taste of the life he wanted when he completed a fortnight's work experience at a funeral parlor. As he entered his adult years, he grew to accept that he didn't have the mental capacity to delve into the field of the dead professionally. Instead, he took a job as a porter at a local hospital, which he loved. Sometimes he got to wheel bodies in and out of the morgue. But the Body Farm, now that really was the cream of the crop.

The Body Farm was a unique place in the U.S. where unclaimed bodies were laid out in the grounds and left to be studied as they decomposed. Crime scenes were constructed to train CSI teams, and at any given time there would be around forty bodies. Steven, who desired to become a part of the scene, had flown from the UK and volunteered as a porter there. Though Dr. Linstrum had found his request to volunteer odd, free labor was free labor and she wasn't about to turn it down. Unfortunately for Steven, just like with every place he'd donated his time, they had found a reason to dismiss him. Perhaps they didn't like his humor.

Standing outside the gates to the farm, shrouded in the cover of night, Steven decided that he'd had enough. This was his dream, and if those bastards insisted on giving him the boot, he'd donate a little something other than his time; something for them to remember him by.

He was aware that there was a huge crime-scene reconstruction already staged for the following morning, all ready and waiting for a brand new batch of trainees. It was meticulously coordinated and organized; severed body parts had been strewn and "murder" weapons had been concealed. The trainees were facing a timed crime puzzle. Well, Steven smiled, he'd just add a little unexpected detail to the mix. Give the apparent "experts" something to really mull over.

After scaling the wall, Steven dropped into the farm and staggered around the tree line, taking care to avoid the security cameras. He burped, tasting the concoction of alcohol he'd spent the last few hours drowning his sorrows with, and proceeded to familiarize himself with the scene before him. It was a double-homicide, both female victims with some of their organs removed. The organs, Steven guessed, were scattered around the ground ready for the training team to locate.

"Sshhtupid Linstrum," Steven muttered, unzipping his jeans and pushing them down to his ankles. He stood there for a moment, swaying proudly with his nether regions exposed, smirking. He took his trusty penknife from his pocket, stumbling a little as he tried to coordinate his hand. With the alcohol and the cold, he was beginning to feel rather numb.

He chuckled to himself as he got to work. His plan was genius, no, inspired, he thought. When the team got there in the morning, they'd go about their simulated investigation. At some point they'd start to solve the murder mystery, and then one of them would stumble upon his donation to the cause. If they weren't going to let him be part of their precious system, then he was going to bring it down, if only for the day. Steven laughed at his amazing idea as he tossed his testes into the trees.

"Figure that one out," he slurred, his smugness enveloping him like a warm blanket. Mere seconds later, Steven realized that it wasn't the warmth of smugness spreading through his limbs, it was a searing pain emanating from his groin. He looked down at his self-mutilated manhood, and let out a whimper. All of a sudden, he wasn't feeling so drunk and all of a sudden, this didn't seem as funny.

He meandered like a cowboy into a clearing where he knew security would see him on their monitors, hoping that at the very least, an ambulance would get to him before he bled out.

And then he heard the barking.

Steven froze, pressing both hands to his modesty, as though the fast-approaching canines would judge him otherwise. How, in all his research about this place, could he have forgotten that this was also where they train cadaver dogs? Cadaver dogs that are also used for security, and released once the silent alarm is tripped because—he had learned this in the first week—only a lunatic would break into the Body Farm at night.

Steven Plunkett was discovered shortly after his demise; he hadn't stood a chance against the dogs. In a small way, however, he had gained a victory. Thanks to the clean up of his own body interrupting the training exercise, his testes hadn't been discovered for four days, really throwing a spanner in the works for the trainee team. Everything ground to a halt as the experts struggled to separate bits of Steven from the planted body parts. Somewhere, Steven groaned—so much for keeping his dignity.

ABOUT KAYLEIGH MARIE EDWARDS

Kayleigh Marie Edwards is a welsh writer, who mostly dabbles in horror and comedy. She has a few stage plays under her belt, and several short stories in various anthologies. She can be found writing articles at www.gingernutsofhorror.com and www.spookyisles.com and can be contacted at ofthedead@hotmail.co.uk

She also loves cheese.

NURTURE
BY K.Z. MORANO

Different species may copulate
but cannot breed.
But we loved each other
and I felt a mother's need
to nurture.
My body kept killing his seed.
So my egg was harvested,
fertilized, replanted
for me to nurture...
But again and again, we suffered
my womb's treacheries.
Pickled fetuses adorn the shelf—
like macabre trophies
of my failure.

He was from a highly evolved species
of Syngnathidae—
with a built-in brood pouch
to carry their progeny.
The suggestion hurt my pride.
But it was our last alternative...
I had no option but to give.
I consoled myself
with thoughts of the future.
Inside my husband's gravid gut
was a precious baby
that I would soon care for.

Nurture by K.Z. Morano

Then he miscarried.
Blood bloomed on the sheets,
red and bright as poppies,
trickling from his birthing hole
in a sinuous crawl.
He let out a mangled cry
when he saw the blob of slimy flesh
with a tiny black dot for an eye.

I flogged myself from guilt
and resentment.
Though the doctors' reptilian eyes
remained devoid of judgment,
I knew they blamed my genetic flaws,
my humanity.
They said the half-human baby
was uncommonly enormous
and that my husband's nursing sac
was not as elastic as my uterus.
Would I be open for a partial hysterectomy?
It would be better, too, they said,
if the ovum wasn't produced by me.
Inside, I protested:
But it wouldn't be my baby...
Not technically.
But it was our last alternative…
I had no option but to give.

So I submitted myself to microsurgery.
They removed part of my uterus
and performed a unilateral salpingo-oophorectomy.
They cut across my pubic bone,
removed one fallopian tube and ovary.
They anastomosed each severed tubal artery
to his distal ileal arteries.

I suffered it all…
the hemorrhaging, the pain,
infections from immunosuppression,
the surgical menopausal syndrome,
and the depression.
They gathered the egg that he had made
and fertilized it with his own frozen seed.
While I became a half-woman
robbed of my right and need
to nurture.
He radiated a glow
that I would never come to know.
I watched his belly
and its growing gibbosity,
and every cell in me grew corrupted
by the maddest kind of jealousy.
A child pulsated
inside his paternal womb
while mine remained hollow,
still as a tomb.

I induced his labor
with intravenous oxytocin.
He let out a stupid scream
as he felt his cervix ripening.
I denied him
of a caesarian delivery
just as he had stolen
everything from me.
The baby was too big
for his birthing orifice.
But it was my last alternative…
He had no option but to give.

I held my husband's manacled hand
as the smashing waves of pain
crescendoed over and over again.
All the while I panted and pushed,
pretending it was me
experiencing the agony.
Giving birth was carnage—
a bloody affair.
His belly—soft and scaly—ripped open;
I heard his muscles tear.
Then my baby's first cries
shattered the air.

ABOUT K.Z. MORANO

K.Z. Morano is a beach bum who writes anything from romance and erotica to horror and dark fantasy. She is the author of *100 Nightmares*, a collection of 100 horror stories, each written in 100 words, with over 50 illustrations. Her stories have appeared in various publications.

She blogs at theeclecticeccentricshopaholic.wordpress.com

Facebook page: www.facebook.com/100Nightmares

BABYMAKER
BY LAYLA CUMMINS

Barren. That's the word they used. My whole life's purpose, gone, just like that. I was surprised, but not inconsolable like some women would have been. Children never appealed to me. Even from a young age, I knew.

But I was in the minority.

We were taught that times had changed. Women had to do their duty by providing the allies with healthy offspring. Future soldiers.

A woman my mother used to know had fifteen children altogether. Women would stop her in the street and congratulate her, or keep their distance, throwing her dark looks and whispering to each other. Women who had only managed to produce seven or eight healthy children before their reproductive organs broke down. When my mother's friend died giving birth to her fifteenth child, her name was added to a memorial in the center of town.

It wasn't always this way. Before my mother died, she told me what life was like for women before the war. They went to work, they drove cars. They were pilots, surgeons and politicians. They chose whether to have children or not. They were free.

*

I am lying on a hospital bed in a private room. A framed poster on the wall opposite shows a muscular woman holding a baby in each arm as a young boy and girl cling to her knees. The caption reads "God bless our Mothers of War!"

The young nurse depresses a syringe plunger in the air and

a squirt of pink liquid shoots out of the end. Satisfied, she leans over and slides the needle into my arm.

"Miss Lee, this will hurt just a little."

Strands of carrot-colored hair fall from behind her ears. I can see microscopic powder particles on her face. "I think what you're doing is *so* noble," she gushes, as though I have a choice.

The law states that all excess bodily tissues are the property of the Government. My defective ovaries can be donated for parts, stem cells or even food in areas of the country where resources are scarce.

"Miss Lee, this will hurt just a little," she says again. Or does she?

I blink. And then I'm alone in a different room. Bigger, whiter, more clinical. A trio of empty beds stare at me from the wall opposite. Pain shoots through my stomach and I instinctively clench my body. It makes the pain worse.

"Hurts, don't it?" says a husky voice.

I twist my head toward the sound and see a girl in the bed next to mine. She's a little younger than me with a pretty face and expertly coiffed brown hair. I realize I am sweating.

"Mine did too, when I woke up," she continues, looking at my crumpled face and slick forehead. "How big's your scar?"

I reach down and push thick covers and hospital gown out of the way until my stomach is exposed to the dry air. I glance down and struggle for breath.

The scar is thick and raw. Dried blood cakes the wound. Giant metal staples hold everything in place. I'm suddenly terrified that I'll cough or sneeze and those staples will pop off one by one and I'll bleed out all over the crisp white cotton sheets. It doesn't look real. It looks botched. I think of old monster movies. Of Frankenstein.

"Yup, it's a biggie," says the girl next to me. "Don't worry about it. It won't look so bad in a few days."

Her name is Caroline. She's been here for more than a week. She tells me about her asshole boyfriend.

"He acted like he didn't know what I was talking about, can you believe that?" she says one evening whilst filing her nails into neat little squares. "But I sure as hell didn't give myself the clap.

"I'm not sorry though. Can you imagine *me* pushin' out a barrel o' kids with these hips? Nuh uh, I don't think so. I'm glad this happened." She puffs a curl of hair out of her face.

She chats while I heal. She tells me her brother's all the family she's got now after their parents died during a rescue mission in Pyongyang, the North Korean capital. "They never believed in no war," she says in her husky voice. "Spent two months protesting outside the ammunitions factories. They nearly pitched a fit when Billy signed up. Course, he came home with one leg less than he went out with, so they couldn't stay mad."

She gets out before me of course. She packs all of her belongings into holdall, except for a tawny fur coat that she drapes around her petite frame.

"You look like a movie star," I tell her.

"Thanks, doll," she grins.

Her brother comes to pick her up. He seems nervous, jittery, glancing around at the empty beds like he's deep in enemy territory. He never quite meets his sister's eye. Caroline introduces us in her singsong way and he mumbles a greeting I don't hear. How different they are, I think.

Caroline and I swap phone numbers, just like our Government-issued pamphlets suggest, but also because we like each other's company.

"I'm gonna miss you, hon," she says, pouting. "You make sure you give me a call as soon as you're out, okay?"

*

It's my turn a few days later. No one comes to pick me up from the hospital, but I don't mind. I like my own company. Always have. A hospital orderly insists on wheeling me down to reception even though I tell him I can walk just fine. A girl with a vacant expression calls me a taxi and I go home.

I make good on my promise and call Caroline the very next day. She sounds quiet, like she's far away.

"Meet me for a coffee?" she asks.

I walk into town, breathing in the cool air. I pass a woman coming up the hill. She's struggling with a twin buggy, one of those mammoth contraptions that can fit a baby and a toddler at the same time. The toddler screams and throws himself against the straps. A natural fighter, I think. His sister is quieter, her big watery eyes staring at nothing in particular. Their mother's face is fat and red, her expression strained. But when she sees me she flashes me a superior smile.

I finally reach the café and spot Caroline in a booth in the corner. I'm grinning—I can't help myself—but my smile fades as I get closer. She's wearing her stunning fur coat but doesn't look like herself. Her skin is the color of sour milk. The bouncing curls in her dark hair have vanished. I slide into the seat opposite and she gives me a wan smile.

"I've been getting sick," she says. "And I've put on a ton of weight." Her eyes dart around the café. I look around too, curious. There's not many people here. A disheveled woman holds a book open with one hand and rocks a pram containing her sleeping child back and forth with the other. I catch a man in a dark suit staring at us. When he sees me, he jerks his head back to the paper.

I comfort Caroline. "I'm sure it's nothing serious." She nods and wraps her tiny hands around her coffee cup. I notice her nail polish is chipped in several places.

*

I was washing dishes when the pain came. I doubled over, nose skimming the kitchen linoleum, screaming my head off. My stomach lurched and I vomited over my new slippers.

"Come back in," said the nurse over the phone. "We'll get you an appointment with Dr. Hart. He's the best." She sounded breezy, as though I'd told her I had bumped my head.

*

I am in agony. The pain comes in waves, a dull ache lapping at my nerve endings, then churning and rising into a tsunami of corrosive acid.

Dr. Hart calls my name and I waddle into his office. He points to a bed covered in thin pieces of hospital paper, and I lay down, panting heavily.

Dr. Hart carries out a battery of tests, checking my temperature, my heart rate, my breathing. Then he puts a hand on my stomach and presses gently. Pain shoots through me again and I grunt, curling up on the bed and trapping his gloved hand between my belly and thigh.

"How have you been feeling recently, Miss Lee? Sick? Tired?" he asks, slipping his hand out.

"Fine, until now," I say through gritted teeth. Dr. Hart nods, like he was expecting this. He sits down in his chair and picks up a clipboard and pen. He scribbles something and signs it at the bottom. Even from the bed I can see his signature; fat, loopy letters, an obnoxious sign off.

"I have some wonderful news, Miss Lee," he says. "You're pregnant."

I stare at him. "That's not possible."

"Oh, but it is. When we removed your ovaries we replaced them with mechanical ones that have been specially designed for women in your...situation." He folds his hands together on his lap. "They self impregnate. And at such speed too. It's really rather incredible." He suddenly clenches his hand into a fist and slams it into his heart. "We *will* win this war!"

"That's not possible," I repeat, my hands out in front of me like I'm warding him off. "What did you do to me?"

"Miss Lee, please calm down."

I make an ungainly break for the door. Two orderlies appear from nowhere and grab me gently but firmly under the arms, carefully avoiding my stomach. A third pricks me with a needle and I fall without hitting the floor.

*

I wake in another room, huge, grey. A factory floor. The walls are beige, the lights are dim. And it's hot. Too hot. There are no crisp white cotton sheets here. Just thick brown leather straps around my wrists and stirrups to hold my feet in the air. Doctors come by every few hours to make sure everything's still in working order.

Caroline's here too, although they give her drugs almost daily now, keeping her under at all times. Without the sedation, her constant sobbing "disturbs the other mothers." Caroline's on her fourth, although I don't know if she knows that.

This lump in my belly will be my third. It would have been my fourth except there was a technical fault and It died somewhere in the middle of its cycle. They have engineers who come and "clean house" before fixing the machines.

I don't know what happened to the first two. I've never seen them. None of us ever do. They are taken away as soon as we push them out without the aid of Government-issued drugs in case it "harms the baby."

A girl who's been here longer than the rest of us says they are groomed for the army. She says that's why we're here, to provide soldiers for the front line. She rubs her swollen belly and tells us all that it's her sixth. The doctors like her. They feel that she helps group morale and has a good attitude, so she is allowed to walk freely around the floor. Every day she'll stop at the foot of each bed, raise her hands up and say "God bless our Mothers of War!" She beams when she says it, but to me her eyes look dead.

Sometimes it's a friend or family member that nominates us, someone who supports the war and knows we're not doing our part. They receive a small fee for their services. Caroline shrieks her brother's name over and over again during those few moments of lucidity, before a nurse comes rushing over to give her something to make her go back to sleep.

Sometimes, when the baby pummels me from inside, I wonder if somebody I knew put my name forward, or if I was simply discovered, if I let my true feelings slip whenever procreating was mentioned, or if-

I reach for the call button.

My water just broke.

ABOUT LAYLA CUMMINS

Layla Cummins is an author, screenwriter and freelancer from Bristol, England and shares her house with her family and three unruly cats. Her short fiction and poetry has been published in *Bugs: Tales That Slither Creep & Crawl*, *Sanitarium Magazine*, *100 Doors To Madness* and online at *The Saturday Evening Post*. Her first ever TV pilot made her a finalist in the Sir Peter Ustinov Television Scriptwriting Award in 2014. She's currently manning the 2nd Reads folder over at Grimdark Magazine and is heading off to Ireland to finish her novel. Check out her website laylacummins. com or follow her @LaylaCummins

GRÄFENBERG FULFILLMENT
BY GIO CLAIRVAL

Dental Assistant Letitia liked her men bald: the muscular and the skinny, the biologist and the forklift driver—any type would do so long as his genetic makeup had predestined him to lose his hair. *Bald is sexy*, she thought. *Bald is virile*.

On the technical side, Letitia welcomed all dental conditions: periodontal pathologies, granuloma, edentulism. Her favorite, however, was the simple cavity. When a patient turned up for his first consultation, the sweet expectation of what she might find made her tremble. Cavities opened the door to her wildest fantasies.

That day, as a bald man staggered into the dental practice, howling in pain, her head swam. She prayed for a carious process, hoping the decay had already developed, affecting the dental pulp. In her opinion, it was the best moment to start an odonto-erotic treatment.

The man (Luka, an art gallery owner of forty-two—she read in his file) sat in the waiting room, hands gripping the armrests. Letitia gassed him with nitrous oxide. Luka let go of the armrests as the gas weakened his socio-immune defenses.

Letitia's following move was to hypnotize her patient in order to induce a classical Lorenz's imprinting. Swing-pendulum-swing. After Luka was brought through from the waiting room, following her like a duckling, Letitia had him recline in a dentist's chair sprinkled with a rutting female bear's scent. The *dernier cri* in pheromone fragrance.

She had previously mixed the anesthetic with an aphrodisiac substance excreted in her own brain—namely, by the serotonin-gorged *epiphysis cerebri.*

The dentist, Mr. Heinz, proceeded to inject anesthetic into his patient's palate, in the most sensitive spot of hard cartilage. Luka, instead of wincing or groaning, let out little moans of pleasure.

"You're... er... very brave, sir." Mr. Heinz cast a puzzled glance at his assistant, who glanced back with Bambi eyes.

Letitia then handed a special amalgam to her unsuspecting boss. "Amalgam" was an old-fashioned word, dethroned by the modern "composite." She however preferred the vintage term, which evoked a scent of forbidden alchemy. The mélange consisted of the usual ingredients enriched with bits removed from her body. Letitia mixed the formula in her quarters. She had a range of specially tailored treatments at hand: the ovarian follicles she kept for her shiest patients; the men afflicted with patchy alopecia received fillings based on piliferous bulbs from her bikini line.

She liked to know that a patient would exit the dental practice carrying a little something of her. Eyes closed, she saw herself experiencing vicarious masculine lives: bar fights, flurries of dirty jokes, fishing tournaments, ball games and muscle car racing, not to mention porn and culinary feasts that even Babette, her favorite restaurant's cook, would never have dreamed of.

And there was more. Letitia sensed when someone touched her bald man. From the depths of the filled cavity, she partook in her patient's sexual interplay. The Sandrized men attained such erotic expertise they all became unparalleled lovers.

Was she content with her invasive practice? She still felt something was missing, a rough-edged cavity in her heart that her soul's tongue could not leave alone.

She sometimes ran into a man who'd been treated at the dental practice with her special amalgam. She would spot him treading High Street, or in a shop, or at a bus stop. The clue that gave him away was the sudden flash of tingling that blossomed in her nether regions, progressed to her nipples and finally reached the scalp in a paroxysm of white-hot shivers.

Each time, the temptation to reveal herself and the secret

of the odontoerotic treatment assailed her, although the dental assistants' strict deontology—already frazzled by her procedures—prevented her from crossing a further line.

Until that very day.

Luka was an attractive man, but it would have been another patient to receive amalgam enriched with the usual parts of her body, had she not noticed a singularity. To counter his receding hairline, he'd shaven off all his hair. She remarked a geometric implantation of the hair growing back on the shaven head.

A perfect rose, starting from the crown, unfurled clockwise, not unlike the pattern of sunflower seeds.

A star-struck Letitia leaned over her patient while, at the same time, tilting the chair back. Now, the dentist's chair had been designed never to keel over. Luka, on the other hand, could flex and contort his body. The generous chest that was drawing close, threatening to press against his face, triggered a sudden movement. The tray supporting dental tools tipped over. Luka, in an attempt to catch something, gripped Letitia's white coat, ripping it, along with the blouse underneath. Patient and assistant fell on the floor among the din of tools hitting the tiles like stainless-steel hail.

An unknown feeling washed over her.

In the dead silence that ensued, "I'm afraid of dentists," Luka murmured. "And I'm truly, truly sorry. Please forgive me, madam. It's my fault."

A few minutes later, Letitia reached for the tiny box that contained an amalgam never used before, a composite enriched with tissue excised from her Gräfenberg spot. The best ingredient. Sublime.

When Luka left, Letitia asked a colleague to stand in for her and exited the practice, scrubs still on.

On High Street, the men stared, perhaps made curious by the white coat open over a half-ripped blouse. But Letitia only ran after Luka. Desperately.

Their encounter, or collision, in front of his house, produced a series of shockwaves.

"You're mine," she said.

"I love you," he replied, unaware of the G-spot inserted in his maxillary first molar (N. 26).

He elbowed the door open; she kicked it shut behind them. They ripped each other's clothes off on their way across the apartment until they lay intertwined under a flashing skylight. Maxilla and mandible interlocked, impervious to the dentist's burr.

The Gräfenberg Spot fired them up in unison. Transplant success.

ABOUT GIO CLAIRVAL

Gio Clairval is an Italian-born writer and translator who has lived most of her life in Paris, France, and now commutes between Lake Como, Italy, and Edinburgh, Scotland, followed by her pet, a giant pike. Her fiction has appeared in magazines such as *Weird Tales*, *Fantasy Magazine*, *Daily Science Fiction*, *Galaxy's Edge*, and several anthologies, including *punkPunk!* (Dog Horn Publishing), *The Lambshead Cabinet of Curiosities* (HarperCollins), *Caledonia Dreamin'* (Eibonvale Press), *Darke Phantastique* (Cicatrix Press), and *Postscripts* (PS Publishing). She can be found at KOSMOCHLOR: www.gioclairval.blogspot.com/ and regularly haunts Twitter as @gioclair

NUTJOB
BY T.J. TRANCHELL

Parker saw them everywhere: red-haired, blue-eyed monsters. Once, a girl of maybe three walked right up to him, glaring at him with an ocean of hate in her eyes, and said, "Daddy." He reached down to pat her on the head, but stopped short. Instead, he scratched himself, feeling the place where the matched set he was born with was now incomplete. It had been that way for four years.

A stupid credit card he never should have signed up for, student loans coming due, and a pressing need to eat every day forced Parker into the sperm donation office. He'd donated plasma before, but that had become a hassle. You had to go twice a week to make any real money and Parker often missed a day and had to cycle back to the beginning. He could make, he was told, as much in one session donating sperm as he could in a month of plasma donations. Parker had nowhere else to be that day, so the sign on the door did not turn him away.

NOTICE:
FIRST TIME DONORS
ALLOW FOR 6-8 HOURS
SCREENING AND PROCESSING

He expected to be looked at like a pervert—movies taught him that this sort of place was perfect for pervs looking to get paid just to jerk off—but the matronly woman at the counter barely looked up as she handed him a clipboard loaded with forms.

"Fill these out and don't lie," she said. "We'll know if you do."

Parker didn't say anything. He took out the pen he always carried (the thought of using a pen held by who-knows-how-many paid masturbators gave Parker the creeps), and sat in the plain white plastic chair farthest from the front desk. Everything seemed to be made out of the same hard white plastic, even the clipboard on Parker's lap. He filled out the form, not unlike the form he filled the first time he donated plasma, but noticed that the section for emergency contacts was blocked off, seeming to make that information more important. Parker had but one word for that section: NONE. He wrote the same word on the line following "Next of Kin" and "Current Dependents." He signed and dated the last line, stood up, walked over to the desk and handed back the clipboard. He gave his "you're welcome" without hearing a "thank you" from the receptionist and headed back to his seat. The waiting room remained empty.

"Mr. Parker," an authoritative voice said before his ass reached plastic. "This way." A woman, with similar, but softer features than the receptionist, beckoned to him from a glass door. Parker tried to admire her figure, you know, to get in the mood, but the shapeless shift—white like everything else—hid whatever curves she had from him. She led Parker down a spotless hall and through another door that Parker didn't even see until the woman opened it.

"Wait here, please," she said and closed the door behind her. The room contained nothing but another chair like the one in the waiting room. The walls, the floor, and the ceiling were all the sterile white that Parker was not getting used to.

He twitched and scratched and waited. His balls itched the worst but he tried not to scratch there. He knew there were probably hidden cameras and he didn't want to seem too eager. After what seemed like an hour, but was only about five minutes, a voice spoke from one of the walls.

"Welcome, Mr. Parker. We're happy you have chosen to visit us." A red square appeared on the wall near where Parker thought the voice emanated. "Please place your hand on the red square, palm down."

The intrusion of color into the blank world didn't so much throw Parker for a loop as it attracted him. He stepped closer to the wall and put out his hand. Immediately he felt tiny pinpricks on his fingers.

"Thank you. The blood test will determine your suitability as a donor."

"How long will that take?" Parker asked, although he could not be sure he was speaking to an actual person.

"Test complete."

"Mr. Parker, we'd like to offer you an enhanced donation option. For a significant upfront payment and subsequent monthly payments, we would ask that you donate more than just sperm."

"How much?" Not *what do you want* but *how much*. Was Parker truly that desperate? No, but he was curious enough to keep his options open.

The red square turned green and some black type appeared within it. The big number was enough to pay off his student loans. With the small number, he could pay off his credit card in less than a year and maybe even afford his own apartment. "Where do I sign?"

"You already have, Mr. Parker."

The white room went black and Parker felt a small stab in his neck. Before he lost consciousness, he felt his shoes being removed and his pants being pulled down.

He drifted in and out of consciousness, at one point telling a disembodied face that he was a red head and needed more anesthesia. A moment later, he thought he heard someone say something about testicles and how he would only need one. He didn't think too much about it. Those big numbers consumed his thoughts and he returned to the darkness.

*

Parker didn't wake up in his own bed because he didn't have a bed of his own. He woke, sore in a particularly sensitive area, on a bench in the park where a little girl would call him Daddy not quite four years later. In his right pocket was a deposit receipt with more zeroes than any other number. In his left pocket, the side that hurt the most, Parker found a roll of twenties, a note with the phone number of a local real estate agent, and a bank account number. At the bottom the note was signed:

Thank you for your kind donation.
- Ilene

Parker felt like a free man, if not a whole one, when the account and the real estate agent checked out. For a year, he lived within his new means and with no debt hanging over his head. The urge to return to the donation center caught him off guard, but going back did not seem necessary. His new account was always replenished on the first day of the month and he never asked questions. Sometimes, he had to scratch himself more than average, but even that was only a minor inconvenience. Instead of going back to the office where he had his left testicle removed—donated to whatever unknown cause the voices behind the white walls served—he went back to the park where he woke up that day.

He sat on the bench—*his* bench—and zoned out. He was glancing toward the twisty slide when he saw a little boy with copper on his head and the summer sky in his eyes. The boy wore black shorts, a Batman shirt and a goofy lopsided smile, and Parker thought he recognized him.

Parker stood up, hoping to see someone chasing after the small boy who could barely walk, but saw no one nearby. Thinking the boy lost and separated from his parents, Parker approached, but as he closed in, he remembered where he had seen the boy before.

It's me. That boy is me. Parker, with no family left alive, has the image imprinted on his heart: him, barely one, showing off his Batman shirt and his crooked, goofy smile. His scrotum tightened, easier now than a year ago without the extra testicle, and he shivered in the heat.

And then he ran.

*

A year later, he was back at the park. He didn't see the boy in the Batman shirt, but he did see a trio of copper-headed toddlers sitting on his bench. He didn't stay long enough to see their faces, to see if their eyes were blue.

*

On the third anniversary of waking up on the bench, Parker tried to stay away, but he couldn't help himself. His scrotum itched and his one remaining ball wanted to be better friends with gravity, pulling him body and soul to the ground. Like the extra space in his scrotum, the bench and the park were empty. He sat down and stared at the twisty slide for an hour before leaving. As he walked through the parking lot, a black mini-van cruised by him. The van was full of little redheads.

He did not see the driver.

*

For the next year, he saw them everywhere: all with steel-blue eyes and hair like polished copper. A glint of pale skin and a few freckles would flash by in a car mirror while Parker waited for a bus. He would see a pair of eyes staring at him from across a restaurant and he would stare back, like looking into the sky. He never saw any adult around these children who all looked like him. He imagined a white wall between each child and the child's guardian, a wall so clean no one could see it, but so solid that Parker's own eyes couldn't penetrate it.

Parker's fourth visit to the park was the first time one of the children spoke to him. Just that one word—Daddy—and Parker wanted to put his hand on her head, but his scrotum retracted, reminding him of the day he went to donate sperm. Parker dropped to his knees and asked the only question he could think of.

"Where's your mommy?"

The girl smiled and pointed to the sky. Parker slumped, making him appear shorter than the girl, and looked to where her small finger actually aimed. An army of three-year-old redheads, all taller than him from his submissive position, swarmed toward him. He assumed they all had blue eyes, but he didn't notice. His own eyes focused instead on the mass of sharp white teeth gnashing toward his softest parts.

ABOUT T.J. TRANCHELL

T.J. Tranchell is husband to an amazing woman and father to an astounding son. By the time you read this, he will have a friggin' Master's degree in literature from Central Washington University and will be enrolled in the Master of Fine Arts in Creative Writing program at the University of Idaho, which isn't too shabby for a dude with a GED. He's been published in *Despumation, Mad Scientist Journal,* and *Niteblade.* His first novel, *Cry Down Dark,* just needs a few revisions and his second, *Good Fences,* was his Master's thesis. He met Michelle Kilmer at Crypticon, which just goes to show how well the network functions.

YIN AND YANG: THE DONOR
BY KATIE CORD

"In a nutshell, do you think it is better to have one nut or two?" I asked him. He looked at me. Tears streamed down his lax face. I swore I saw a twitch of his mouth. He needed more succinylcholine. I wanted him to stay loose, but able to feel the procedure. It was an important part of the therapeutic process. If my hypothesis was correct, my new surgical technique would solve all the world's problems.

I patted his cheek, "Now, now, my little sweet. Your life will be so much better. No more staying up all night masturbating to pornographic material, no more wanting to dominate woman, you will live good life. I guarantee it."

He gurgled as words tried to come out of his mouth. I connected the syringe to the IV line, his breathing slowed, his mouth went limp, his stare fixed ahead. I wish I could be so lucky to have someone help me with my part, but as it has been since the beginning of time, the woman must bear the brunt of the pain.

Slicing your own skin is difficult if you have not practiced for many years. I started cutting myself to calm my urges of self-harm when I was a young girl at the boarding school in Switzerland. It seemed so far from my home in Belarus. I always felt so alone. It is a talent, curse, and blessing to feel this isolated.

In the beginning, I made mistakes. The mind, it gets nervous it makes you cut too deep, too shallow, you never know what you are capable of when the adrenaline pumps. But, when the mind is disciplined, you can cut yourself to the depth you want and anyone else for that matter. Of course, going to medical school helped me immensely. You can only learn so much from experimenting on yourself and lab animals. I personally don't like hurting animals. They do nothing wrong. They are pretty balanced. Humans? Not so much.

Not like this schmuck.

"Damn it," I said aloud. I scanned the room for a fresh scalpel. I'd already used four today.

It is difficult not to keep cutting on something when the sweet rush comes. I didn't want him to be mutilated, but in case he had a surge in hormone, I wanted the behavioral modification to kick in. Ah, sometimes, it is very easy to forget that my donation must be made before I can start the procedure on the patient.

The laboratory, torture chamber, pleasure room, site of multiple murders, tit for tat, anyway, the patient designed this room for his comfort. Not mine, not the woman he lured in here. Just for him. It is not like being in surgical suite. That would be easy. I sort of wish I had American associates who could help with this procedure, but even my friends in Europe do not agree with my theories. It leaves to have to do this on my own. But that has been my whole life.

I look over at my patient one last time, his calculatedly fractured femur will set in a way that he will never chase woman again. The missing thumb on his right hand will ensure he never snatches another girl by her hair. The microscopic scars on his face a warning to all that he is marked. I don't want to intubate him so I must hurry now.

I sit semi-reclined in the dental chair, a mirror focused on my abdomen. I try not to think about what has potentially happened in this chair. I've sanitized it the best I can, but old blood stains the white thread and cracks in the vinyl. Bright surgical lights are necessary so that I can see the microscopic vascular system of the ovaries. I want to keep the fallopian tube intact. The lights cause a halo effect when I look away. I must remember that when the pain starts so that I know I'm not hallucinating.

The brown of the betadine wash cools and stains. A

laparoscopic procedure would have been ideal. I could puncture through the skin, snake my way through, cauterize and nip what I want, but I will do this the old fashioned way. I wipe away the excess betadine and take a deep breath. The procedure will be done in breaths. Inhaling, I place the scalpel to the lower right midline of the suprapubic area. Exhale, I slice vertically with pressure enough to go one inch under the skin. The initial slice does not hurt; it is when the air hits the open edges that I want to scream.

Inhale.

Exhale. I cut along the one inch line about three centimeters, just large enough to put my hand in.

Inhale.

Exhale. I cut through the subcutaneous fat. Let me tell you, dieting to the point this would be easy was a very frustrating experience. Even with the starvation, the abdominal fat is still layered two centimeters deep.

Inhale.

Exhale. I slice through the tough fibrous abdominal fascia. Between, deep breaths, I tuck the retractor under the fat, muscle, and gently over the small portion of the intestine poking out.

Inhale.

Exhale. I tug upwards holding the retractor in place with a pulley of my own creation.

Inhale. I visualize the infundibulopelvic ligament, underneath will be the small life-giving orb.

Exhale. I clamp the ligament with a one-centimeter bridge in between clamps.

Inhale.

Exhale. I cut between the clamps, transecting the ligament with a pair of Mayo scissors. Inhale.

The room becomes black.

A moan, it is soft at first but begins to crescendo. I open my eyes and reorient myself to the room. The blood has pooled on my abdomen like a makeshift mud puddle. The shock of seeing my own organs must have set in. The clamp is still in place locking off the main artery of the ligament, but there are other arteries bleeding and without suction it is a mess.

Thump.

He's starting to move.

I must finish the procedure quickly.

I grab the sterile towel and sop up the blood. It seems like an eternity before I can visualize the surgical field. It takes all of my intention to breathe slowly. My heart is racing. I've lost just enough blood for my body to respond without my permission. I check the clamp again, insuring that it is not causing the bleeding. I transect the fallopian tube and ovary from the uterus with my scalpel. I need to cauterize the tiny vessels, but they will have to clot on their own. The thuds of my heartbeat are making concentration difficult. The ovary and fallopian tube come out with a slight tug of the forceps. I look at the round pink orb. The tube is intact. Perfect. With luck, it will attach to the spermatic cord without issue.

"You fucking bitch, when I get up from here, you're going to wish I would kill you." His words were venomous, but he was still in four-point restraints.

"Oh my sweet, you think you can hurt me?" I said. Coy had always been my favorite way to play. I tried not to pant, but it is very difficult when the heart races.

Sloppy work has never been a favorite thing of mine. Yet, ensuring the patient meets his therapeutic goals is most important to me. I stuff sterile gauze in my wound, padding the clamps in place until I have sedated the patient and finished his procedure.

Four large sutures are used to close the wound.

Thump.

I jump.

He is kicking with his good leg.

I tremble for a second.

Now, I'm angry.

No one makes me tremble.

No one.

I push myself to sit up. For a moment, I put an oxygen mask

on, cranked up to 15 psi, and push two milligrams of morphine into my thigh.

Yours is coming, you stupid disgusting pig.

After five minutes of pure oxygen and morphine, a person can start to feel whole again after a procedure. The headache will be a pain in the ass later.

I walk over to him. I grab the vial of Ativan, draw up eight milligrams, and mix it with succinylcholine.

Without thinking, I screw the syringe onto the IV tubing and push the plunger.

Damn, he's going to be asleep for the procedure.

I was smart enough to set up the sterile field before I worked on myself. Of course, my original intentions were to be alert, with minimal pain, and completely whole while performing the procedure on my patient. Instead, I'm standing here with blood leaking out of my abdomen with a clamp held in place with gauze. I must work slowly and replace a radical orchiectomy with a simple one.

In short, I'm going to cut his nut out through his ball sack.

His face is limp, his breathing slow. He gets to be at peace while I heal him from his demons.

I cleanse the scrotal sack with betadine; I'd already shaved the testicles and pubic area. He'd had a slight erection from the closeness of the blade. Sometimes, his type gets aroused from danger to self, even if his favorite way is to hurt others. I wipe off the area with sterile gauze then use it to pull the scrotal sack tightly. I slice a small incision then use my Mayo scissors to cut it open. You would think the testicle would just pop out, but it doesn't. There are layers of fascia that must be sliced through and it is of importance to clamp off the main artery of the spermatic cord or he will bleed to death.

I don't want him to die.

The lights are making me sweat. I can feel the dampness on the back of my neck. But, I am cold. My fingers feel prickly.

I have to finish what I've started.

I cut the ligament cord, and tug. The clamp holds. I search for the main artery in the ligament so I can attach it to the one from the ovary.

Anatomically, the male and female are so similar yet different.

Every piece on the body had its own modification related to hormones, genes, and these two little matching organs in our body.

The G-spot? It's where the prostate should be.

Those elegant folds of skin called the labia, just a prettier scrotal sack that tightened up.

Yet, I would never do what this pig has done over and over to multiple women. Yes, many men have died for my scientific discoveries. This one will not die.

My pulse is in my throat.

Soak up the blood, there it is. I take the ovary and fallopian tube and attach them to the spermatic chord. Artery to artery, vein to vein, I make tiny, tight stitches. It reminds me of my grandmother teaching me to quilt. She was beautiful, mysterious. Many a woman would come to her with difficult medical concerns they did not want a doctor to find out about. I remember helping her by digging holes and placing small shoeboxes in the garden.

The ovary's color starts to return.

I turn up the volume of normal saline infusing into the patient. The ovary tucks nicely beside her new partner. I start to stitch the scrotum back together. I will return to check on my work after I fix myself.

Myself. My heart is beating so fast. I hear the panting but I don't even feel it anymore. I have to put down the needle and driver.

I feel like I have urinated on myself. I look down. My scrubs are completely bloodied in the front.

I grab the side of the table and slink to the floor. The panting continues. My heart is racing so fast I can no longer move.

It is suddenly quiet except for a weird ringing sound in my ears.

I close my eyes.

The last thing I hear is, "What the fuck have you done to me?!"

I whisper. It is all I can do. "I have balanced your demons. I have given some lightness to your dark."

ABOUT KATIE CORD

Katie Cord lives in the Pacific Northwest with her three rambunctious dogs. She's a nurse by night and writer/publisher by day. When she has free time, she likes to spend it with her boyfriend, Tim. She is the owner of Evil Girlfriend Media, and the author of *He Left Her at the Altar, She Left Him to the Zombies*.

THIS LITTLE PIGGY
BY M. LORI MOTLEY

Nicole sat at the edge of the bed and fiddled with the collar of her fuzzy, purple robe. No cheap cotton gown for her. Two hours into the hospital stay and her mother had already run back and forth three times to fetch things she just couldn't live without. She stood near the corner smiling vapidly and staring at the side of her daughter's head.

I clutched the thin, cotton blanket over my ribs and sat there, consumed with fear about whether I should move my leg away or actually dare to lean it against her hip. It was my bed, after all, and she was here to thank me.

She flashed a smile. It wasn't one of those smiles I fell in love with the year before when we had Algebra 2 together, but a disconcerting mixture of appreciation and I-would-rather-be-anywhere-but here. Her well-wrapped foot swung a few inches above the floor. She did that in Algebra all the time too, with her shoe dangling from her pink-tipped toes.

"Thank you," she said at last.

"It's not like anyone would give me their toe. Even if they really have to like you do." The smile dropped away from her face like a stone vanishing in a murky pond before she bolted upright and limped toward the door.

*

An hour after Nicole had gone, I was still mentally scooping up bits of myself and putting them back in place. The blanket had slid off my feet and I caught a glimpse of my pale toes. "Soon…"

I whispered like the evil guy in every horror video game ever. A shiver wormed its way up my spine.

*

Period four, Nicole and I shared Chemistry lab. I sat two tables away and watched her swing her foot and giggle with her crew. The supply cabinets lined the wall behind her and I took every opportunity to grab new test tubes or Bunsen burners. My Bunsen burner must have mysteriously stopped working ten times that semester. That day she had chosen bright blue sandals and she sat there, swinging her foot with one strap caught between two perfect toes tipped with pearly pink polish.

I stopped looking where I was going. I tripped over nothing and the Erlenmeyer flask in my hand went flying. It arched through the air in slow motion, tumbled toward Nicole and her friends, landed just so on the swinging foot, knocked the blue sandal to the floor and crashed down on her other foot.

"You jer-" Nicole's best friend Madeline jumped up and turned on me like a rabid cheerleader.

And then the screams started.

I looked down at the glass shard ruin of the flask, to the blue sandal upside down on the tile and to Nicole's other foot with the little toe smashed and severed and lying in a spreading pool of blood.

My vomit hit Chad McGovern, right guard of the Fighting Hornets. I knew, when all this was over, no matter what I did to make it better, he would still beat me up.

"You owe her, you little ferret," Chad said as he slammed my head against the lockers again. "You have no choice. Get that through your head."

"Fourteen pairs of shoes she can't even wear anymore," Madeline snapped at me when she caught me scuttling to the bathroom after lunch. "How can she get a pedicure now without those little nail techs babbling about it in whatever language they speak?"

Before the week ended, knots of people followed me between classes, crooning, "Here little piggy..."

Explaining to my parents had been the hardest part. How do you tell parents that you need to give your little toe to the head cheerleader so her boyfriend doesn't kill you? Honor, though. *That* they understood. I had to do it since it was my fault she lost her toe to begin with.

*

The flat yellow light of the hospital room made time stand still in disturbing ways. I glanced down at my foot and wiggled my toes. Still all there. My hand brushed over the squashed blankets where Nicole's rear had rested, but I couldn't tell if they were warm or not. I wondered vaguely if there was still some way to get out of this. Then I heard her voice echoing, *it's not like just anyone would do it*, and wondered if we could just get it over with.

After a long time in which the flat yellow faded to gray and then back to yellow again, the doctor and one nurse with a huge chest and bad teeth pushed into my room and posed at the end of my bed like American Gothic. The doctor looked familiar.

"Sign this," the nurse said and leaned over to thrust a clipboard at me.

I signed it, not caring what it said at this point.

The doctor and I stared at each other. I frowned. The idea that I knew him from somewhere wouldn't go away.

"Lock the door," he said to the nurse and she plodded across the room to obey.

I saw now that they had come in with a rolling cart. A small metal dish and some random scalpels and scissors lay spread out like some ancient king's cutlery at a museum. That worm of fear came back, creeping up and down my spine with its thousand tiny feet.

With a nod from the doctor, the nurse moved hurriedly around the bed now. From nowhere, wide straps appeared. The sudden *brrraaap* of loosening Velcro turned the worm into a snake.

One across my chest before I could even think about sitting up. The nurse's thick-fingered hand clamped around my right wrist and strapped it tight to the bed rail.

"Hey... hey. What is this?" I jerked feebly on my hand and watched the nurse plod around the foot of the bed, her dark eyes trained on my face.

"You signed the form," the doctor said and folded his hands, waiting.

The nurse shot her hand under the blanket where I had been hiding my other hand and wrenched it toward the bed rail.

"Wait a second," I said, but another *brrraaap* sounded and another strap bit into my left wrist. Another strap across my waist, one at my thighs and then each ankle trapped and restrained with swift, sure movements.

The nurse stood next to the doctor again, a smirk growing on her face. "He does have those pretty toes though, doesn't he? Wears socks to bed, this one." She rocked forward on her squeaky white shoes and chuckled. Her chest, trapped as it was in the too-tight scrubs, shook like California.

"Let's begin then," the doctor said and turned aside to choose a scalpel from the tray.

"Whatever you say, Dr. McGovern."

My mind tripped over itself. Begin? What did they mean, begin? And then, McGovern? Oh no. A sudden mad thought, *I wish I didn't drink so much Hi-C at lunch*, flew through my mind as I peed myself.

"Please," I squeaked. "Dr. McGovern... Chad's dad? Please, sir. I'm doing what I'm supposed to do!"

He bent over my foot, scalpel poised and descending. "Nicole is a very sweet girl. Chad is very fond of her," he said to no one in particular.

I screamed. "Help! Someone help me!"

But the nurse lunged for my head and leaned over, squashing my head into the pillows with her chest. For a second I couldn't breathe, then managed to turn my head enough to suck in a few shallow breaths. Struggling was impossible. "Ooh, boy. I think he's crying." The nurse chuckled again and shifted herself into a better position on my head.

*

My parents told me I was brave and such a good boy for doing what I did. They told me I'd be a hero and pushed me back to school. The marching clumps of kids following me everywhere were gone. Now they leaned back against their lockers, hands over their mouths and laughed.

I slipped into my chair in the chem lab, eyes on the scarred table in front of me. Chad's deep guffaw drifted across the room at me. Nicole's golden giggle joined it like the twist of a knife. I couldn't help but shudder.

"Quiet down now," Mr. Franklin said and started in on the periodic table again.

Halfway through the class I caught myself staring at that swinging foot. Her toe… my toe… was a bit too long and still red around the base. The nail was hot pink and peeking out from the straps of a white sandal.

Chad McGovern caught me looking and snarled. I tore my gaze back to the surface of my lab table and tried to ignore the slow throb of where my toe used to be.

Nicole didn't even glance my way.

ABOUT M. LORI MOTLEY

M. Lori Motley constantly suspends the reality of suburban life by climbing out of this world's neat boxes and into worlds of fantasy and horror. Learn more about her published works and current projects at www.MLoriMotley.com.

VICARIOUS
BY CHRISTINE MORGAN

It started with the blood drive.

The community blood drive, the one they held as part of the fundraiser and relief effort for all those people affected by the disaster.

I felt bad for them. Of course I did. To watch that kind of suffering on the news, to read about the losses of homes and loved ones, to see the devastation and damage.

I felt bad for them, and I did want to help. I sent money to the charity, and, under other circumstances that might have been the extent of it. What else could *I* do, someone like me? Join the sponsored walk?

But there was the blood drive, and they had it all set up outside the library. The whole Red Cross thing, with the white tents, and the bloodmobile.

If it had been at the hospital, or the clinic, or the plasma center, I probably wouldn't have gone. Not downtown. Not unless I had to.

At the library, though, that was another matter. I mean, I was going there anyway. It's one of my safe places, and part of my treatment plan. To get out of the house at least once a week, you know? The library's where I go. It's quiet, it's calm. Besides, I can check out books and videos. I have a little cart on wheels and I fill it up. They have lots of travel shows, nature documentaries, that sort of thing.

If I'm really having a good day, I might—*might!*—even detour through the park on my way back. Sometimes the tiny local farmer's market is happening. If it's not too crowded, and if I can stand it long enough, I'll bring home some fresh flowers or produce.

That day, though, it was the blood drive.

It was anything but packed. Which was too bad for the volunteers, waiting around bored, but better for me. I saw them on my way in, spent the entire duration of my time in the library trying to psych myself up, and then on the way out I gathered every bit of my nerve and went on over.

I'd never donated blood before. I'd had it taken for medical tests, but never donated. They were very nice. Very gentle and friendly. If they could tell I was nervous, it must not have seemed strange to them. I just didn't explain how it wasn't the sight of blood, it wasn't the needles, it wasn't anything like that. The poke didn't even hurt.

I felt good after. Like I'd done something useful for once. Like I'd contributed to society, like I'd helped in some small way. An old lady who reminded me of Aunt Gretchen gave me a cookie and a cup of juice, and I went home.

Of course, later that same day there was a mixup with my grocery delivery and I had to call the store, talk to the manager, and then deal with a substitute driver who treated me like a freak, so, I had a rough evening and a worse night despite taking an extra pill.

The next week or so, I didn't think about it much. I still saw the news, and I had pasted my heart-shaped "I Gave Today!" sticker on the fridge as a reminder, but it seemed more and more like something I'd read about than something I'd actually done.

Then …

Well, then the strange stuff began. Not spooky-strange, but weird-strange, unfamiliar-strange. I'd be sitting right there at home, in my chair like always, and I'd get these … I don't know what to call them … impressions, feelings, sensations.

As if daydreaming, only I wasn't. As if dream-dreaming, but I was awake. Deja-vu, but not. A sort of ghost-echo-mirror, reflecting experiences that weren't my own.

For instance, I'd be inside with the shades drawn, alone in the cool darkness, but have this sense of being outside, in the fresh air and warm sun.

I realized—and I know this will sound crazy, but, bear with me—that it must have been because of the blood I'd donated.

That blood was given to someone else, and part of me had mingled with part of that person. Or those people. Could have been more than one; I have no idea.

Whoever, though, and however many … we were connected. We were sharing.

Or, at least, I was. I can't imagine it was a two-way effect, not from just a pint or whatever of my blood in their veins. Nobody contacted me about it, not then, and not later. Funny; isn't it usually the other way around in the horror movies? The recipient is usually the one troubled by visions, foreign memories, phantom sensations.

I shared these ghost-echo-mirrors of their moods, their movements and actions and emotions and activities. I'd never had so much as a sip of alcohol in my life, but I finally learned what being drunk was like. I felt their adrenaline rushes, the good, heart-lifting kind that comes from excitement and anticipation, instead of the gut-wrenching kind caused by anxiety and fear. I felt their comfort, contentment, relaxation and relief.

I felt *alive*. Alive, and glad of it. Like life wasn't a tedious, grueling and grinding obstacle course just to get through the day. Like life really was something that could be enjoyed, even reveled in.

Which I knew it was, obviously, but it took more courage and confidence than someone such as me would ever have.

On my own, I'm a timid, terrified, paranoid mess.

This gave me the chance to, in however small a way, experience so much more.

It was wonderful.

I could be *safe*, and still feel *alive*.

The trouble was, it didn't last. It wore off. Maybe blood gets assimilated and recycled, and so the effects faded. Soon, all too soon, I was only my old self again.

Only, in a way, that little hint of something greater made being just my old self again feel that much worse. I'd had a taste, a glimpse, a sample ... then lost it ... and missed it more than I would have believed.

I gave more blood. I made as regular a habit of it as the blood bank would allow. But it wasn't always needed. The results weren't steady, couldn't be counted on. I never knew when or if my blood might be used.

So, I decided to investigate other options.

There are groups that let you donate your hair, you know. To make wigs for women who've gone bald undergoing chemo, that kind of thing.

Well, I hadn't been to the beauty shop since Aunt Gretchen died, and my hair was down past my waist. I forced myself to go, got it cut short, and donated it to one of those groups.

It didn't work. Not for me. Hair's dead, after all. Strings of dead cells. I suppose it made a fine wig, and that some lady was happy to have it, but I never felt a thing one way or the other.

The bone marrow registry, though ...

Yes, the extraction procedure hurt like hell, and yes, it had to be done at the hospital downtown. I've never been such a nervous wreck. But it was worth it. Oh, it was so, *so* worth it!

Her name's Tessa, the little girl I was a match for. She was five. Five, and crippled by a deadly disease. What kind of world does that? Despite it all, she was cheerful and sweet. Her family adored her. She loved ponies. She had lots of friends.

My bone marrow saved her. Made her whole, healthy, and strong.

It took a while, of course, and during her recovery period we were both pretty miserable, but as she improved, it was the best feeling I could have imagined. She wrote to me, too, sent me a thank you card and crayon drawings. When her parents took her to Disneyland to celebrate her clean bill of health, it was like I was right there with her.

I'd never been to Disneyland. The rides, the fireworks, meeting princesses, hugging Mickey ... it really was magical. I'll never forget it. She sent me a postcard from there, too, and a snapshot of her in mouse ears.

In none of her letters, or those from her family, was there any single hint that Tessa might be picking up anything from my end, sharing my experiences. That's another reason I'm convinced it's not a two-way effect.

Then there's Jacob. He has my kidney. You only *need* one, right? The blood transfusions might wear off, and I didn't know if the bone marrow would eventually do the same. An actual organ, however, that seemed like something that would be there for keeps. So, I figured, what was the harm?

I first learned about him online, one of those viral share-this-post things about the teen swimmer whose Olympic hopes might be dashed if he didn't get a new kidney. I put myself on the prospective donor list right away, thinking that even if I didn't end up with Jacob, I'd be bound to help someone.

I could hardly believe it when Jacob's doctors contacted me. They did want to fly me to Boston, but once my own doctor explained my situation, they were more than willing to make every accommodation. The surgery was done right here in town, at our own hospital. Stressful, sure, but compared to having to travel? To a huge, strange, crowded city? I wouldn't have been able to do it.

Flying *is* awfully neat, I have to say. I don't know why so many people are afraid of airplanes. At least, it's neat the way I've experienced it. Maybe if part of me goes with someone who is afraid of flying, it'll be different. I get to try a lot of things I otherwise never would. I've been skydiving *and* scuba diving, how's that for exciting? All without leaving the safe comfort of home.

Those were with Mark and Arlene, though, and I was talking about Jacob. The skin grafts came later.

Living vicariously through Jacob is amazing. It's almost sensory overload. A teenage boy, an athlete, he's just all energy and action. He's got a girlfriend, which makes things kind of awkward sometimes, but he's much more focused on training right now.

I hope he makes the team. I'd love to go to the Olympics. Wouldn't that be incredible? I've watched it on TV often enough, but to be there ... the parade of nations, the opening ceremonies, the competition ... and if we won, oh, how would that feel? Standing on the platform, still wet from the pool, the weight of the medal, the cheers of the crowd, the thrill as the anthem plays ...

Makes you shiver just thinking about it, doesn't it?

Where was I? Oh, right, Mark and Arlene. The skin grafts. Mark was a burn victim. Arlene had skin cancer. *Those* were some seriously painful procedures and recoveries all around, let me tell you. But, again, worth it. They're both such good people.

Mark works with animals now, rescuing dogs that would otherwise be put down ... so, in a way, I'm helping them, too. I like dogs. I can't have one, it wouldn't be fair to the dog to be cooped up with me. Dogs need more of a social life. They need walkies and runs at the dog park and trips to the vet.

As for Arlene, she's the outgoing type, active in her church, married thirty years, three grown children and two grandkids. Her bake sale specialty is apple-spice cake with cream cheese frosting. I've made it myself, using her recipe. Melt-in-the-mouth delicious.

I wish the liver transplant had worked out for Felix. He wasn't an alcoholic or anything like that. And his body didn't reject the tissue. There were other complications. I think the hospital bungled the surgery and then covered it up so they wouldn't be sued. Poor Felix. I didn't have the chance to get to know him well, but I was with him when he died.

I sometimes wonder if I should write to his fiancee to tell her that he didn't suffer. I did, not being under any anesthesia or on any drugs at that point, but he didn't.

The liver regenerates. Isn't that bizarre? They can cut out a lobe of it, and within a few weeks it'll grow back, and be back to full normal functioning. Mine did, perfectly fine. I take good care of myself. I eat right, I exercise, I don't smoke or drink on my own. I'm a great candidate.

Which is why it should make sense to let someone keep donating! It's a renewable resource, like blood and bone marrow, replenishing itself, but it's also an organ like a kidney. Over time, a single donor could share bits of liver with dozens of people, *dozens!*

All those lives …

All those experiences and sensations …

I mean, yes, there's books and movies, there's video games, and there'll be those virtual reality simulators some day. But imagination, high-def, 3-D, great graphics, and surround sound can only do so much. It's not the same, is it? Not the same as doing something for real.

And if someone can't do something for real, why's it so wrong to want the next best thing? Especially when, at the same time, you can help other people? Save other lives?

I don't think it's that unreasonable. I think it's better than reasonable. I think it's good and noble and right. Everybody wins!

My doctors are the ones being unreasonable. Some of them had the gall to suggest I'd developed more mental problems, and suggested I undergo addiction counseling.

Addiction counseling!

When I've gone off my post-op pain meds well ahead of schedule after every single surgery, thank you very much! I don't want to be all numbed and clouded. I want to *feel*, though when I told them that, they looked at me like I was turning into some sort of masochist.

They don't understand.

They won't let me donate any more. Not even blood.

As if I'm supposed to just go back to the way I was. As if I'm supposed to live like *this*. This limited, restricted existence.

When I could live so much more.

More deeply, more richly. More fulfilling.

So much *more!*

It'd almost be a kind of immortality, wouldn't it?

And generosity. The ultimate generosity. Think how many more people I could help. How many other lives could be made better.

That's why I've researched traumatic brain injury. I know just what to do. I know just how to do it. To leave the most parts undamaged and viable. Heart, lungs, corneas, stem cells, limbs, bones. Anything they can harvest. Anything they can use.

They'll probably try to call it suicide, but that's just stupid.

I'll be more alive than ever.

ABOUT CHRISTINE MORGAN

Christine Morgan works the overnight shift in a psychiatric facility, which plays havoc with her sleep schedule but allows her a lot of writing time. A lifelong reader, she also reviews, beta-reads, occasionally edits and dabbles in self-publishing. Her other interests include gaming, history, superheroes, crafts, cheesy disaster movies and training to be a crazy cat lady. She can be found online at www. facebook.com/christinemorganauthor and christinemariemorgan. wordpress.com

FLIGHT PATTERN [PART ONE]
BY TARA ROBERTS

At 1:17 in the afternoon on June 14, 2014, a male American robin (*Turdus migratorius*) weighing 3.4 ounces and with a slash of yellow across its distinctive red breast, dove for a common earthworm (*Lumbricus terrestris*) curled in a patch of clover on the administration building lawn at North Snake River Community College in Patchley, Idaho, and whether it was the erratic wind speed that day or a flaw of genetics that dampened the bird's depth perception or something else entirely, the robin never met its prey, but rather drove itself beak-first into the right temple of 28-year-old administrative assistant Callie Marie Peterson (*Homo sapiens sapiens*), which on a good day would cause a nasty headache, and on a bad day might bruise the temporal bone just under the skin, and on a really bad day might fracture the temporal bone and lead to bleeding from the ear and vertigo and maybe even a little leakage of the cerebrospinal fluid, but on this particular day cracked the temporal bone and blasted apart the malleus behind it and ruptured not only Callie's ear drum but also the inch-wide saccular aneurysm that had been sitting, undetected and asymptomatic, near the corpus collosum of her brain for six months, causing her to drop dead right there on the lawn in the sun.

And maybe the bird would have missed her if she'd packed a lunch that day instead of deciding to walk to Taco Time, or if she'd stopped to go the bathroom first, or if she hadn't been avoiding Lisa from across the hall because of the incident with Lisa's husband at the Christmas party, or if Lisa had married Trevor Mills from high school instead of her husband, or if Callie's college boyfriend hadn't hooked up with their biology professor, or if Callie's mother had married a nice farmer in Nebraska instead of running off for godforsaken Idaho, or if Callie's great-grandmother had died of yellow fever on the way out to Nebraska instead of her little brother, or if the ship that brought her great-great-great-grandparents from Düsseldorf by way of the Netherlands had hit the rocky outcropping at the head of the bay, or if the leader of some obscure northern European tribe had succeeded in defeating the invading Goths, or if the land bridge to Alaska had stuck around a little longer, or if a certain mango tree had failed to thrive and left a certain family of small primates to starve, or if the earth had coalesced a few thousand miles closer to the sun, but the fact of the matter is none of those things happened and all the things that happened did and the entire course of the universe up to this point led to the bird striking the girl on the lawn, which is pretty much a big giant miracle if you stop to think about it for a second, which Callie, of course, never had time to do.

So Lisa saw the collision as she ate lunch alone at her desk and called the ambulance, which arrived in 4.7 minutes, precisely the average response time of ambulances in Patchley, Idaho, and the volunteer EMTs put Callie on a backboard and rushed her to the hospital even though, as one of them put it later, it was pretty damn obvious things weren't going so hot, and after all that could be done was done the attending physician declared her dead and called her mother back in Nebraska and her father and his girlfriend Jessica in Palm Beach and confirmed Callie's organ donor status by the sticker on her driver's license, and the ambulance, swift but with less fanfare this time, transported her body on ice to St. Thomas Medical Center in Spokane, Washington, where a surgeon who still longed for the Netherlands of his childhood guided a team as they removed and prepared and packaged a litany of Callie's organs and tissues, excluding her damaged right middle ear bones but including her pristine left ones, the globular malleus and arced incus and delicate stapes, which were soaked in saline and reshaped... [to be continued in TAKE: An Anthology of Anatomical Entries]

ABOUT TARA ROBERTS

Tara Roberts lives in Moscow, Idaho, with her two unruly sons, patient husband, and odd poodle. She is a lifelong Idahoan and studied creative writing at the University of Idaho, where she now works as a science writer.

MORE FROM WHEN THE DEAD BOOKS

WHEN THE DEAD

There is no way out for the residents of Willow Brook Apartments. Outside a plague is spreading while behind the walls, neighbors are forced to become friends…or enemies.

When the Dead…will introduce you to a doomed family, a dying child, an egomaniac, a murderer, and many other undesirables (including the undead!!) in three floors of secured-access chaos.

THE SPREAD

You don't know when it will change your life, or how, but the zombie plague is spreading quickly and in ways that no one could have imagined.

Featuring short stories that showcase the many ways in which a disease can overwhelm a city, The Spread will get you thinking of how mundane acts can become deadly.

LAST NIGHT WHILE YOU WERE SLEEPING

Displacement, replacement, injection, rejection, the best and the worst birthdays ever, vengeful spirits, disgruntled bridge trolls, a semi-sappy Satan, Bloody Mary as you've never seen her, Bigfoot, a suburban brush with the undead, rainbows you don't want to find the end of, and more.

This collection includes mostly dark and sometimes humorous poetry, flash fiction, and short stories from the mind of Michelle Kilmer, including 'Mirielle', a finalist in the Crypticon 2014 Writing Contest.

LAST NIGHT WHILE YOU WERE SLEEPING also features illustrations by talented artists including Rob Sacchetto, Nick Gucker, Kriscinda Lee Everitt, Travis Bundy, James Lacroix, and others.

whenthedead.com facebook.com/whenthedead @whenthedead

Made in the USA
San Bernardino, CA
12 June 2015